WATSON
—— ON THE ——
ORIENT
EXPRESS

The series page at Amazon:
amzn.to/2s9U2jW

THE **SHERLOCK HOLMES/ LUCY JAMES** MYSTERIES

WATSON
— ON THE —
ORIENT EXPRESS

BY **ANNA ELLIOTT**
AND **CHARLES VELEY**

This is a work of fiction. Names, characters, organizations, places, events, and incidents are either products of the author's imagination or are used fictitiously.

Typesetting by FormattingExperts.com
Cover design by Todd A. Johnson

ISBN: 978-0-9991191-8-1

"Who is't can read a woman?"

—William Shakespeare
Cymbeline, 1623

SATURDAY, JULY 9

1. LUCY

"Are you sure you're up to taking on another case?" Jack asked.

We were standing at our front doorway, waiting for Mycroft's carriage to arrive. From behind us in the kitchen came the clink of silverware as Becky finished her breakfast porridge, punctuated by an occasional woof from Prince. Becky had a habit of sneaking him scraps of bacon under the table.

"You don't think I'm fit to investigate another man's disappearance?"

Jack had to leave soon for Scotland Yard and was already in his blue sergeant's uniform. "Do you want the honest answer, or the one where you're still speaking to me at the end of this conversation?" He smiled briefly, but I could see the shadow of worry in his dark brown eyes. I couldn't blame him. Ours was a dangerous profession. Jack, as a police officer, worked within the law, while Holmes and I, as private consultants, worked alongside it—or sometimes skating along its outskirts. But in both our lines of work, allowing your mind to be distracted could prove deadly, and the truth was that we were all of us distracted right now.

Watson had been kidnapped two days ago, and despite the combined efforts of Scotland Yard, Holmes, and every one of the Baker Street Irregulars whom Holmes employed, we still hadn't a clue where he had been taken. Or even whether he was dead or alive.

Jack must have picked up that thought, because he said, quietly, to avoid Becky's overhearing, "Odds are he's still alive. If they'd killed him, someone would have found the body by now."

"I know." It was true, and a reason for hope I was willing to cling to. But I'd been held a prisoner by one of our more unpleasant enemies just a few short months ago, and my imagination kept painting unhelpfully vivid pictures of what Watson might be suffering, even as Jack and I stood here talking about him.

I shook my head, trying to dislodge an image of Uncle John chained up in the dark. Or bloodied and bruised from torture. One of the reasons I'd agreed to accompany Mycroft and Holmes to the Harwell family estate in Kent was that I had already done everything possible in the search for where Watson was being held. The enemies who had taken him knew exactly who I was, and it wouldn't shock me to learn that Jack, Holmes and I were all being discreetly watched when we left the house. The Irregulars stood a much better chance of finding a clue to Watson's kidnapping than I did, and in the meantime, being forced to think of something else for a while sounded more appealing than staying trapped here with my own churning thoughts.

"Mycroft wouldn't have asked for help if the matter wasn't urgent," I told Jack. "I don't think it will be dangerous, just a matter of questioning Lady Harwell about her husband. For all we know it may be nothing more sinister than boredom with domestic life. Lord Harwell may have gone off to the South of France to lie on the beach of some seaside resort and swill champagne."

"If it were as simple as that, Mycroft wouldn't be involved," Jack said.

That, unfortunately, was also true. A shadowy figure in the British government, Mycroft Holmes had, over the years, spun a web of influence that ranged from finance to domestic security to foreign policy and treaties between warring nations. His cases never proved simple, and this one was unlikely to be an exception. From what little Mycroft had told me over the telephone, Lord Harwell had been a lower-level diplomat with the Foreign Office.

"I'll be careful," I told Jack.

"It seems like I've heard that before. Oh wait, it was probably just before you decided to confront a blackmailer and got stabbed. Or the time you were scaring a confession out of a murderer and got shot at—"

"I know, I know. I don't know how you stand me."

Jack reached out and caught me in a hug. "Lucky for you, you're worth it."

For a long moment, I shut my eyes and let myself lean against him. But then the rattle of carriage wheels came from just outside. "That will be Mycroft. I'll take Becky with me so that we can drop her off in Baker Street with Mrs. Hudson." I drew back enough to look up at Jack. "You'll keep an eye on the beat constables' reports that come in? If any patrols find—" I couldn't quite make myself say the word body, but my mind flashed on an imaginary picture of Watson's lifeless form, floating in the Thames or lying somewhere in a muddied ditch.

"I will." Jack squeezed my hands. "Now go help Lady Harwell find her husband."

2. WATSON

A brilliant white flash of light. It shone once, twice, three times. Three brilliant white flashes, each accompanied by a sharp, popping sound.

I shut my eyes tightly against the glare, although I felt a strange lassitude. I smelled something. Chemical smoke.

I heard a man's voice. I thought I recognised the harsh tone. He said, "That'll do."

I was lying on my back on something firm. My skull throbbed. Where was I, and how long had I been here? What was the last thing that I could recall? Three burly men, forcing their way into my consulting room past my horrified assistant. No words. I had grappled with their leader, until a push from another one spun me round. Then a fierce impact at the back of my head.

So that would explain the throbbing.

I heard footsteps walking away. Clear sound echoing off hard surfaces. The footsteps were on hard tiles. A wooden door closed. A medical facility, I thought. Or a morgue. I was on a gurney.

I moved my arms slightly, testing for restraints. I could not feel any straps. I nearly opened my eyes, but then came another voice from across the room. I knew that voice.

"He still breathes." It was Lord Sonnebourne.

A hot surge of anger rose in my chest. I had to stop myself from tensing, lest my captors realise that I could hear them. I had encountered Sonnebourne in his riverfront mansion several weeks ago with Holmes and Lucy. The man led a powerful criminal organization called The Sons of Helios, which specialized in helping wealthy criminals disappear. Holmes had been pursuing one of those criminals, a murderess named Mrs. Torrance, since January. In July, less than a week ago, Holmes had been poisoned and nearly killed while investigating another of those disappearances. We were certain that Sonnebourne's organisation had been responsible.

I had treated Holmes for the poison and left him resting at Baker Street to return to my surgery. Shortly after my return, the three burly men had attacked me.

Had Holmes also been set upon and captured?

Another man's voice. A coarse, East-end accent. "Still sleepin.'"

"How long?"

"Midnight was 'is last injection. Another half hour."

"Wake him then. When he is able to speak, bring him to the interview room and then come back here. I want you to watch him through the portrait and report on whether he is truthful."

"Do you want me to soften him before I bring him in?"

"Only after. If he has not cooperated."

"Understood."

"Now, Clegg, I want you out of this room."

"What about our friend 'ere?"

"Didn't you just say he would sleep for another half hour?"

A pause.

"Now. With me."

Another pause.

Two sets of footsteps on cold hard tiles. Then Sonnebourne continued, "Lock the door."

I heard the click of the lock, and Sonnebourne's voice, muffled by the door. "And keep away from the interview room."

Was I alone?

Of course you are, Holmes would have said. If someone else was still here and able to observe through the portrait, why would Sonnebourne have ordered Clegg to get out?

Still, I was cautious as I took a quick glimpse to my right. I saw a straight-backed wooden chair and beyond it a bare white wall and a black-painted door. Another glimpse, this time to my left. A table with surgical implements and several bottles, and wooden shelves laden with more bottles along the wall. Behind the shelves, a crack of daylight showed between heavy drapes that covered a tall wide window.

No one.

I raised my head slightly. A sharp pang and throb came from the back of my head, cheek, and upper lip. I touched each spot gingerly. No bones broken, I was sure of that. I wondered what I looked like. Then, touching my upper lip again, I realised that my captors had shaved away my moustache.

A portrait of Lord Sonnebourne hung on an otherwise barren white wall roughly ten feet in front of where I lay. What had Sonnebourne said?

Watch him through the portrait.

I sat up. My trousers and boots seemed different somehow. Perhaps newer? Or was this the effect of whatever drug my captors had used to render me unconscious for—however long? I did not even know what day it was. I put my hand in my waist-coat pocket and felt the metal heft of a pocket watch. I withdrew the watch. It, too, seemed unfamiliar. There was no date, but the second hand moved, so it appeared to be working, showing the time to be 7:45. Was it morning or evening?

How long until Clegg would re-enter the room?

I swung my legs over the edge of the gurney and stood. It took me a moment or two to get my balance. The effects of the injection, I thought.

I shuffled to the portrait as quietly as I could manage. I ran my fingertips over the painted canvas surface. At the side, where black oil paint framed the image, there was a view-hole. I pressed my eye to the opening. A lens of some sort was just inside, as if a telescope probed through the wall into the next room. I wondered what concealment on the other side masked this spy device. Then I jerked back in surprise, at a crackling voice that erupted beneath my chin.

"… in the Pera Palace," the voice said.

I saw a telephone earpiece, fastened at the base of the portrait frame.

Keep away from the interview room, Sonnebourne had said. How long did I have until they came to wake me? I pressed my eye to the opening, resolved to learn whatever I could in whatever time I might have.

Sonnebourne was behind a desk, facing me. On the other side of the desk with his back to me was a dark-haired man in a white suit. I could not see his face. The man's hair was long and glossy, as though oiled with brilliantine.

Sonnebourne was talking. "Your room has been reserved and paid for. You need only claim the package when you arrive. And this is for your travel." He slid a fat white envelope across the desk. "Pounds, francs, and liras."

The man glanced inside. "Should be enough."

"And here are two images. They will remain here. You must commit both faces to memory."

The man leaned forward.

"The photograph shows the primary target. A high official in the French government. We receive no payment if he remains alive. Do not return if you fail."

"I will not fail. What about this other gentleman?"

"A matter of retribution. He took something from me."

"He will be in Constantinople as well?"

"Protecting the French official."

"The sketch looks familiar."

"It is an illustration from *The Strand*. The man's name is Sherlock Holmes."

3. LUCY

Two hours later, I was recalling Jack's words and doubting that Lady Harwell in fact required—or at least desired—any assistance. Her rose silk tea-gown was of the very latest fashion, and trimmed with yards of lace that must have cost approximately what Jack earned from Scotland Yard in an entire year. But studying her, one had the uncharitable thought that she looked like the pig dressed up in baby's clothes from Alice in Wonderland: aged somewhere about forty, plump and doughy-looking, with close-set blue eyes, an upturned nose, and a pudgy face marked with the lines of habitual discontent.

Her husband had been missing for several days, but she seemed to take his disappearance less as a source of worry than as a personal affront.

"Really, it is most inconsiderate of Gerald. Most inconsiderate indeed."

We were in the front parlor, which was large and elegant with high ceilings and a Grecian frieze on the walls. The drawn curtains cast the room into semi-twilight. Bright sunlight, we had been informed, sometimes brought on one of Lady Harwell's headaches.

Lady Harwell herself reclined on a velvet-covered divan. So far in studying her, I had been able to detect no signs of actual ill-health beyond what you would expect from a lack of exercise and a steady diet of chocolates and other sweets. But she appeared to be one of those women who turn fears for their health into a hobby. On a table beside her were three half-empty boxes of caramel creams and Turkish delight, as well as an array of little jars and bottles of smelling salts. She now raised a lace-edged handkerchief and touched it delicately to the corners of her eyes, her upper lip trembling with indignation.

"I can't imagine what Gerald can have been thinking of, going off like this without a single word. He knows that my health won't stand the least upset. I mustn't be worried or inconvenienced in any way; it's dreadfully bad for my heart. Any strain sends me straight into having palpitations, and with Gerald gone, I've had to do everything for myself."

Given the number of servants employed on the Harwell estate—so far in the course of our visit I had seen three gardeners, a butler, a footman, two housemaids, and a parlor maid—I doubted that Lady Harwell was ever required to lift one of her exquisitely manicured fingers. But having already treated us to a lengthy discourse on the subject of her heart, she now continued without the least trace of irony. "Would you believe that one of the under-gardeners sent in white roses for my breakfast tray instead of pink ones, and I was forced to go outside and speak to him about it myself?"

"Exhausting for you," Mycroft agreed. There was more than a touch of irony about his tone of voice, but Lady Harwell appeared completely oblivious.

"Exactly! In all of this dreadful heat, too, I might easily have had sunstroke!"

Mycroft interceded before she could expand on that theme. To avoid prejudicing our minds in advance, or so he said, he had briefed Holmes and me only minimally on the drive here.

Beyond telling us that Lord Harwell's diplomatic assignment had been centred around Egypt, he had said very little about the missing man. But watching Mycroft with Lady Harwell now, I was fairly certain that he had never met either Lord or Lady Harwell in person before this.

"When was the last time that you saw your husband, Lady Harwell?" Mycroft asked.

"It was ..." Her brow puckered in an effort of remembrance. "Now let me see, it was on the twenty-fourth. I remember, because that was the day the fishmonger delivered soles for our supper, but I couldn't fancy them at all. I told Gerald that I thought I might be able to manage a few oysters, but he flatly refused to send Bertram—he's our second footman—into the village to fetch some. He has no consideration for my health!" She applied the handkerchief again. "No idea of what I suffer."

I was also by now re-evaluating my hope that interviewing Lady Harwell would prove a welcome distraction from worrying about Watson. At the moment, I felt as though my last fraying nerve would snap if I heard her mention the word palpitations one more time.

Holmes had already escaped, ostensibly to question the servants about their master's having vanished. But I wondered whether his patience was as thin this morning as mine.

"Did your husband seem worried when last you saw him, or had he been troubled recently?" I asked.

Lady Harwell looked nonplussed; apparently having to consider the feelings of anyone else was a novel experience for her. "I don't know," she said finally. "I overheard him shouting at someone over the telephone last week. Something to do with some outlandish foreign city or other."

Mycroft's expression didn't alter. Only if you knew him very well indeed would you be able to tell that Lady Harwell's final words had caught his attention.

"A foreign city? Do you recall which one?"

"No. Only that it began with a B. Or was it a C?" Lady Harwell flicked a dismissive hand. "I really can't be sure, I only remember thinking that it was somewhere my health would never allow me to travel on account of the heat. And of course, the dirt—really, some of these foreign countries have absolutely no concept of proper sanitation, or so I have heard—"

"Quite so." Mycroft cut in adroitly. "Do you know to whom he was speaking?"

"I've no idea."

"And there is nothing else that you can recall? Did your husband ever … ah … discuss any matters relating to his work at the foreign office with you?"

From the dubious tone of Mycroft's voice, he shared my opinion that Lord Harwell would be more likely to march across London Bridge dressed as a clown. But the question had to be asked.

"Oh, Gerald never spoke of his work to me," Lady Harwell said. "He knew quite well that all those difficult foreign names and all the talk of complicated treaties and such might bring on one of my headaches. But he had been working longer hours of late. So inconvenient, because on several occasions it forced me to have to hold dinner until he came home, and once the roast beef was quite dried out and it disagreed with me dreadfully. But my husband was a very hard man. No compassion in him, even when I was awake half the night with pains in my stomach and flutterings around my heart—"

Fortunately for my own sanity, Mycroft interrupted once again. "And we must not risk straining your health any further by continuing to trespass on your hospitality, Lady Harwell. Perhaps you might ask one of the servants to escort us to your husband's rooms so that we may look through his belongings?"

4. WATSON

I stared through the portrait spy-hole at Sonnebourne as he spoke to the dark-haired assassin. My face flushed hot with anger. They were planning to kill Holmes!

Sonnebourne went on, "When you have finished, arrange your own return passage. Stay away from London for a month. The repercussions will be extensive."

"Understood." The voice was nasal, but businesslike, smooth, calm, confident.

"Now take the next train to Dover, then the boat to Ostend. From there, the Wagons-Lits train to Paris. From there—"

"The Orient Express."

"Quite so. The funds in the envelope will cover your expenses."

The man was about to stand, but Sonnebourne stopped him. "And one more thing."

The man froze, halfway to his feet. "Yes?"

"Before you leave Constantinople, shoot the Torrance woman as well."

"Who?"

Sonnebourne slid another photograph across his desk. "She will be somewhere near the Frenchman, possibly amongst his bodyguards, or near Holmes. Likely she will be looking for you."

"I am surprised. She helped me in—"

Sonnebourne's voice cut in, hard and cold. "She is working for Holmes."

The other man leaned over the photograph for a moment. Then he said, "As you wish. It will be done."

Both men stood. The interview was over.

My heart pounded and a thousand questions filled my mind. Holmes, providing security for a French official in Constantinople? And working with the Torrance woman, the murderess we had been seeking for nearly half a year? I would have thought he would have had her arrested immediately, the moment he had found her. But working with her? And saying nothing to Lucy or me?

No, that seemed impossible.

But yet, I had to admit, Holmes had always played a lone hand. Besides, time had elapsed since I had seen Holmes. The Constantinople matter might have arisen after Sonnebourne's thugs had abducted me. Holmes might also have located the Torrance woman during that time.

But why would Holmes work with Mrs. Torrance?

Suddenly I saw the connection.

Sonnebourne.

If Mrs. Torrance was to be in Constantinople, and Sonnebourne had arranged my kidnapping …

Holmes might want her help, both to protect the Frenchman, and to locate and rescue me.

But was I correct in my reasoning?

I realised that I could not waste precious seconds trying to understand the implications of what Sonnebourne had said. I had to escape. And in a few moments the man called Clegg would return. He would expect to find me still asleep.

I had one chance.

I moved away from the portrait and waited beside the door, keeping away from the doorknob.

It was less than a minute before I heard a key turn in the lock. The door opened.

A stocky man in a white laboratory coat stepped inside. He was looking away from me.

I hit him from behind, striking the back of his neck with all the force I could command. He went down hard and fast and most important, quietly. He lay on his side. I recognised his close-cropped hair and meaty, slab-like face, now slack-jawed and unconscious, and felt a moment's satisfaction. He was one of the three men who had abducted me from my surgery.

I hurried to the window and pushed away the drapes. I could see outside.

Daylight.

At least I knew it was morning, and not evening.

I was on the ground floor. The window overlooked a road and a park beyond. The park looked vaguely familiar. Had I been in the area before? Or were these lingering after-effects from the drug that had kept me incapacitated?

Then I caught myself. No time to think or puzzle. I returned to the man I had knocked down and rummaged briefly in the pocket of his lab coat. I found a card case with cards bearing a name: *Clegg*. I also found a key to the door through which he had entered. I locked the door from the inside and pocketed the key, returned to the window and drew back the heavy curtain. The window was of the French style, really a double door, and it was locked. I tried the key. It worked. The door opened.

I stepped through onto the gravel border between the house

and the lawn. I was free. I closed the window and re-locked it from the outside, then hurled the key as far away as possible into some bushes.

The road between the park and where I stood was busy with a flow of carriages, trams, carts, and the occasional omnibus.

I knew one thing. I had to get back to Baker Street, or to a police station where I could telephone Holmes.

Along the road, a hansom cab clattered by at a leisurely pace. I thought of hailing the cabman.

But did I have funds to pay him? I patted my trousers pocket, where I keep my wallet. It was not there. Inside my jacket pocket, however, I could feel an envelope thick with papers. My fingertips brushed over a wax seal.

Where had that come from?

I was on the point of pulling out the envelope and breaking the seal when I saw, on one of the cross streets that ends perpendicular to the park road, a uniformed policeman on foot patrol, wearing the familiar helmet and swinging his baton. I felt a surge of relief and even exhilaration. I would make my way to him and explain everything. He would take me to his police station. I would telephone Baker Street from the station to let Holmes know my whereabouts and warn him of Sonnebourne's plot.

If Holmes had not already left for Constantinople.

I ran towards the policeman. A young dark-haired fellow with a drooping moustache, he stared at me.

"Where am I?" I felt foolish but had to ask the question.

"Why, Lavender Hill, Sir. That's Clapham Common over there."

"Take me to your station. I must make a most urgent telephone call to Sherlock Holmes."

"You better follow me, then."

He turned around. Then he paused. "Better walk in front of me, sir. You're not looking very steady on your pins, you know. Station's about a half mile."

We had gone perhaps two or three blocks when he said, "Turn left, sir. This here's Gowrie Road. Bit quicker."

I looked behind, wondering if we had been followed, but Clegg was nowhere to be seen.

"We're about half-way, sir," the policeman said.

I nodded and set out once again, picking my way along a narrow, trash-littered walkway between decrepit row houses. Few people were on the pavement, but several loungers slumped on the front stoops. They took no notice of us. Still, I was glad that I had the policeman at my back.

Then I felt a rush of wind behind me, and something hard connected with my skull. I saw only darkness. For one fleeting moment the void seemed, somehow, familiar.

5. LUCY

Three quarters of an hour later, we were back in the carriage that had driven us to the Harwell estate in Kent. Mycroft took up nearly the whole of one seat, while Holmes and I sat in the one opposite.

Mycroft waited until we had rattled down the poplar-lined drive and were back on the turnpike road that would return us to London before regarding Holmes from under half-lowered lids.

"Now then, Sherlock. Your impressions?"

Holmes drew his pipe from an inner pocket and tamped tobacco down into the bowl. I could see the marks of his anxiety for Watson in the lines of strain around the edges of his mouth and the grey shadows beneath his eyes. If he'd slept more than a handful of hours since Watson's kidnapping, I would be astonished.

But he responded without pause or hesitation to Mycroft's question. "My impression—backed up by the testimony of several of the Harwell House servants—is that Lord Harwell and his lady are both singularly unpleasant people. They are strenuously disliked among their staff, he perhaps even more than she, and their servants stay on only due to their willingness to pay first-class wages. The gardener to whom I spoke had a wealth of unflattering epithets to apply to Lady Harwell regarding her dissatisfaction with a nosegay of roses on her breakfast tray earlier this week. Evidently, she used a quibble over the roses' colour as a basis for threatening to fire him from his position. 'Fat ruddy harpy' was the least profane of the terms which the gardener used to describe her. Now, as to the missing man himself," Holmes went on, "I will pass over the usual particulars of height, weight, etcetera, which you no doubt have been able to infer as well as I. To begin, then, Lord Harwell is a man of expensive tastes, prone to attacks of gout, likely due to over-indulgence in those tastes. He is fond of claret wine, and imbibing several glasses of the beverage after dinner frequently sends him stumbling up the stairs to his bedroom. The scuff marks on both the toes of his evening dress shoes and the carpet on the stairs were quite distinctive. He has an equally strong predilection for gambling on the races at Epsom Downs and has had the misfortune to back several losing horses of late. His hair is thinning, which is causing him increasing alarm. He has a sportsman's affection for dogs, but a horror of cats."

"Capital, Sherlock, capital." Mycroft rested both hands on the top of his walking stick and regarded Holmes across the space of our carriage, his eyes slightly narrowed. "Really, I have very little to add. Beyond the facts that he has recently dismissed his valet and hired a new one, that he suffered an accident in childhood that left him with a slight weakness in his right leg so that he walks with a limp—oh, and of course he recently visited a dentist in Harley Street to have a tooth extracted."

Holmes put the tips of his fingers together. "His right incisor, surely."

There was, I knew, a strong tie of affection between the Holmes brothers, but one-upmanship in the matter of logical deduction was also inevitable when the two of them were involved in the same case. Some of their deductions I could follow—such as Holmes's observation about Lord Harwell's fears of baldness, as demonstrated by the ten different brands of hair pomade I had counted on his dressing table. As to others of their conclusions, I had to admit frankly that I had no idea of the clues that lay behind them.

"She was the one who brought money into the marriage," I put in. "Lady Harwell, I mean. Lord Harwell may have the ancestral title and estate, but she is the one with a fortune large enough to keep the estate maintained."

Holmes's eyes unfocused briefly in concentration, then he nodded. "The wedding photo of the two of them on the parlour mantle," he murmured. "Well spotted."

"Thank you."

In the photograph, Lady Harwell's wedding gown and veil had been of the same outrageously expensive, flawlessly upper-class make as the clothes she had worn today. Lord Harwell's morning suit and top hat, on the other hand, had been clearly new, but of decidedly inferior quality: cheaper imitation goods masquerading as the genuine article.

I didn't add that Lord Harwell had almost certainly married Lady Harwell for her money; Holmes and Mycroft would un-doubtedly have reached the same conclusion. I also didn't men-tion the small assortment of pristine, entirely unused children's books I had seen crammed half-guiltily away at the bottom of one of the parlour bookshelves.

I did feel a prick of sympathy for her, though. Married to a husband who had probably gotten bored with her five minutes after their wedding photo had been taken. Wanting children, but never having any. And women of her class were never trained for or encouraged in any kind of profession, either; her parents would have died in a collective fit of horror if as a girl she'd ever mentioned wanting to attend university classes or find a job.

It was in many ways no wonder that the Lady Harwells of this world now found nothing better to do with their time than lie on a sofa eating chocolates and complaining of their own ill health.

"And now," Holmes said, "Perhaps you will be so good as to tell us, Mycroft, why Lord Harwell's disappearance is a source of so much alarm."

"And what Constantinople has to do with the matter," I added.

Both Holmes and Mycroft looked at me. There was little resemblance between the Holmes brothers, but now their brows were lifted in identical expressions of surprise.

"Lady Harwell said that the name of the city she heard her husband mention began with either a B or a C. And that it made her think of heat and dirt and crowding. Lord Harwell's diplomatic assignment was Egypt, but she would surely have remembered if the city was Cairo. Even if her husband never spoke to her of his work, she surely would have heard the name before. Constantinople isn't especially close by, but it is in that part of the world and the next largest city with a name starting with C. And you clearly wanted to know very much whether Lady Harwell had overheard anything more than just the name of the city."

Mycroft nodded acknowledgment. "Lord Harwell was not personally known to me, save by reputation. I may say that based on that reputation, I had grave reservations about his fitness for diplomatic assignment. But unfortunately, my opinions are not always heeded at the foreign office. Of late, our government has been working to finally resolve the ambiguities left in the treaty governing the Suez Canal, the majority interest in which, as you are no doubt aware, is owned by France. Lord Harwell was in possession of details regarding a secret meeting that is being organised in Constantinople for that purpose."

"And you believe that to be the cause of his disappearance?" Holmes asked. "Whether because he has turned traitor and decided to sell the state secrets of which he is in possession, or because a foreign power has kidnapped him in order to extract those same secrets?"

"Precisely. And although our visit to Harwell House was informative, I cannot say that it has tipped the scales of my opinion substantially in one direction or the other. Harwell may be a traitor to his country. He may be dead or a prisoner. I should say that either possibility is equally plausible."

6. WATSON

I woke with no idea where I was or how long I had been unconscious. I was aware of a hard bench beneath me, and a cold stone wall that I was slumped against. Faint grey light came from a small window above me. I blinked. Saw the iron bars.

To my right was a metal door, painted grey, with a small view-portal, opened. "Where am I?"

I heard a voice, a man's and only barely respectful. "Lavender Hill Police Station, of course. You don't remember being arrested, Lord Harwell?"

I said, "I wish to make a telephone call."

A young inspector unlocked the door and escorted me to an interview room at the rear of the station. Inside the room was a massive oak table and several chairs. A door with a window led to the street outside. A telephone hung on the wall. I moved towards the telephone, about to lift the receiver.

"A few questions first, Milord," the inspector said.

"Such as?"

"You might start by explaining how you came to be found unconscious this morning, with two dead men, in the alleyway behind Gowrie Road."

"I know nothing about that."

"Nothing about Gowrie Road, Milord?"

"I was walking near there when someone struck me from behind. Then I woke up here."

"Why were you walking near Gowrie Road, Milord?"

I shook my head. It ached with a dull throb. The effects of the blow, I thought. "Do not address me as 'Milord,'" I said. "I am John H. Watson, M.D., friend and associate of Sherlock Holmes. And I must telephone him immediately."

In answer, the young inspector produced a thick envelope with a broken wax seal. "Taken from your coat pocket, Milord."

From the envelope he extracted three letters, all addressed to a "Lord Harwell." In the envelope there was also a thick wad of bank notes in varying currencies. Pounds, francs, and others. "Do you recognise it?"

"Yes, but I do not understand how it got there."

"The initials 'GH' and your tailor's name are embroidered into the lining of your coat. Do you not recognise them?"

I glanced at my inside coat pocket. "I do not."

"Can you explain the letters?"

I looked over the letters. One from a grocer, one from a florist, and one from a haberdasher. All demanded payment for past due amounts. All addressed to Gerald, Lord Harwell, of Parkchester, Kent.

"If I can speak with Mr. Holmes," I said, "all will be made clear. I expect he will come here directly, and that he will bring Police Commissioner Bradford with him. Both of those men know me by sight."

The inspector's eyes widened for a moment at the Commissioner's name. "Very well." He indicated the telephone box on the wall behind me, next to the outer door. "I shall afford you some privacy for your call."

And with that, he left the room.

It was Becky who answered the telephone.

Unfortunately, she informed me, Holmes was not at home. Neither was Lucy. Still more unfortunately, just as I started to give Becky my instructions, the door to the outside opened.

A burly man in a dark blue constable's uniform rushed in and shoved me away from the telephone. The receiver clattered against the wall. I recognised the man called Clegg, although he no longer wore a white laboratory coat. To match his dark blue uniform, he wore a constable's helmet. He gave an evil smirk.

"Now I get a bit o' me own back," he said.

My frustration took over. I leaped forward, taking him by surprise, and drove the heel of my hand into his chin, knocking him against the wall. I hit him again, a solid left hook to the jaw. He went down.

The outside door was still open.

Looking back on my actions, I see that I was functioning on a level of low cunning, for when I saw Clegg unconscious on the floor of the Lavender Hill police station, I shelled him out of his constable's jacket, put it on over the coat I was wearing, and donned the policeman's helmet. Then, on an afterthought, I pocketed the envelope with the cash and walked outside, leaving the three tradesmen's letters behind.

No one stopped me.

I had a moment's exhilaration when I realised that I was free. Clad in my uniform, I might go where I liked. And I had plenty of money in my pocket. I flagged down the first hansom cab that presented itself. "Baker Street, cabbie," I said.

The man nodded. "Right you are, Guv. You want the Chelsea Bridge? Or the Albert?"

"Quickest route," I said, settling back into the seat of the hansom. I shut my eyes, suddenly exhausted. At Baker Street,

I would tell Holmes. What would he want to know? Of course. The facts. I should be prepared with the facts.

But the moment I focused on one thing it flitted off to make way for another. I was tired, hungry, and still feeling the effects of whatever drugs remained in my system.

Again, I tried to focus.

Flashing lights.

A portrait with a spy-hole.

A fight with a burly man named Clegg.

I shook my head. What had happened to me?

Thugs had abducted me early Tuesday evening. From my surgery.

I had awakened from a drugged sleep this morning, on a table, in a building that I later learned was outside Clapham Common.

I had overheard Lord Sonnebourne make plans with a sleek-haired assassin, going over details. The man would receive his weapon and ammunition at the Pera Palace, in Constantinople. That sounded like a hotel of some sort. While there, he would kill a high official of the French government.

He would also kill Holmes. And that I could not allow.

Sonnebourne's final words echoed in my mind:

"Before you leave Constantinople, shoot the Torrance woman as well. She will be somewhere near the Frenchman, possibly amongst his bodyguards. Likely she will be looking for you. She is working for Holmes."

If only I had been able to deliver my message before Clegg had knocked me away!

But "if only" never served to help. What did I know that could be useful?

Well, I did know that Holmes and Lucy were not at Baker Street. So, perhaps Holmes had already left for Constantinople.

Whitehall, I thought. Mycroft Holmes would know. He would also know which French officials were now in Constantinople. He could send a message of warning to Holmes.

I could ask for Mycroft at the Diogenes Club. Ought I to tell the cab driver to go there?

The wheels of the cab clattered on the cobblestones. The summer air, already warm, was getting warmer. The street was getting crowded. I felt dizzy and uncomfortable. How long had it been since I had last eaten?

We had slowed for a crowd near Victoria Station.

Holmes is frequently chiding me for seeing without observing. Observation of the smallest details and understanding their importance requires a state of heightened awareness that comes naturally to Holmes but to me requires more effort. Yet today, with my mind in a drifting, hunger-deprived wobbly state, I saw something that changed my destination and indeed the course of the adventure.

7. LUCY

We were re-entering the environs of London, having passed by the Canary Wharf and the India Docks. Despite the hot summer weather, the grey, grim poverty of Whitechapel and the surrounding neighbourhoods was beginning to close in. No matter how perfect the weather, sunshine and fresh air never seemed to touch the crumbling tenement houses of the East End.

We were passing by a particularly vile-looking building where a pair of drunkards appeared to be trying to pummel each other to death on the stoop outside when a boy's blond head appeared directly outside Mycroft's window—the owner of the head having taken a running leap to perch on the carriage's rear boot.

Mycroft, for once startled out of his usual sedate calm, jerked backwards with a half-uttered cry of surprise. But Holmes leaned forward, his expression instantly alert. "Ah, Flynn. You have news for us?"

Eleven years old, skinny, and invariably looking as though he had rolled head-first through a coal scuttle, Flynn was the leader of Holmes's band of unofficial investigators known as the Irregulars. I knew that Holmes had him pounding the London pavements for any word about Watson—not that Flynn would have allowed himself to be occupied in any other way. He shied away from all expressions of sentiment as vigorously as he avoided soap and water, but he was fond of Watson. "Did you give him a crystal ball in order to keep track of our movements?" I asked Holmes. Probably I should just be happy that Becky hadn't been trawling through the East End's most crime-ridden neighbourhoods with him. The two of them were most often to be found in one another's company, but today for a wonder, Flynn appeared to be alone.

At Mycroft's direction, our carriage driver pulled towards the side of the road and drew to a halt.

"Nothing so esoteric, I can assure you," Holmes said. "I merely alerted him as to the probable route we would take to and from Kent, and told him to keep watch for us in case there was news. Well, Flynn?" Holmes added, as Mycroft opened the door to the carriage, allowing Flynn's entrance. "You have something for us?"

"I do." Flynn bobbed his head, still fighting for breath after running to catch our carriage. "Not that you wouldn't 'ave seen it for yourselves soon enough, but I figured as 'ow you'd want to know about it first thing. Special edition. Just came out this afternoon."

He drew a folded sheet of newspaper from the grubby pocket of his trousers and passed it to Holmes, who spread it out on his knee, then sucked in a quick breath of air.

The sheet had been torn from the front page of a newspaper— the London Times, if I was recalling Holmes's tutelage on the distinctive type setting of the various papers correctly. But that was an unimportant side issue compared to the headline that screamed across the top of the page in letters half an inch high:

Fugitive Wanted for Double Murder.
Have You Seen This Man?

And below, in grainy newsprint reproduction but still instantly recognisable, was a photograph of Watson.

* * *

Shock was still drumming through me as I mounted the steps to 221B Baker Street. I was alone. Holmes had gone to the Lavender Hill police station in Clapham, from which Watson was supposed to have escaped, planning to obtain—although demand would likely be more accurate—information relating to Watson's arrest.

Mycroft was pulling all the weight and influence he could manage with his contacts at the London Times in order to find out where they had gotten the photograph of Watson. For it was a recent photograph, taken in the last few days. None of us recognised it as one that had been taken of Watson before this, and besides, the photograph showed that his moustache had been shaved, and we could see a slight nick on Watson's upper lip and a bruise on his cheekbone that must have come from the attack that had led to his kidnapping.

On the one hand, the photograph might prove that Watson was alive. On the other, our enemies had contrived to have him arrested and turned into the focus of a country-wide manhunt, which didn't—

The door at the top of the stairs flew open, snapping off my train of thought, and Becky's small form came barrelling through, blond braids flying out behind her.

"Lucy! Lucy, I've been waiting and waiting and waiting for you to come back!" She was breathless, her cheeks flushed and her blue eyes bright with impatience.

"I know, I've already seen the papers," I began. "Flynn met us, and—"

"No, not that!" Becky interrupted. Her words were almost tumbling over one another. "I saw the afternoon papers, too, and Dr. Watson's picture and everything, but, Lucy, that's not what I need to tell you, listen!" She took a breath, then plunged onward. "Lucy, Dr. Watson telephoned here! This morning, just after you left. Mrs. Hudson was busy in the kitchen when the telephone rang, so I went to answer it, and I heard Dr. Watson's voice!"

"Watson was able to telephone here? What did he say?"

"He scarcely had time to say anything." Becky took another breath, her eyes brimming with sudden tears. "He just said, 'Hello, is that Becky?' and I said, Yes, it was, and I started to say how glad I was to hear that he was all right and that we'd all been looking for him, but he said, 'I'm sorry, my dear, but I haven't much time, and this is terribly urgent. Is Holmes there?' I said no, that no one was here except for Mrs. Hudson and me. And Dr. Watson said, 'It's vitally important that Holmes know what I've learned about the Or—' and then he stopped." Becky gulped, swallowing. "I heard a hard thump—as though something had fallen, or maybe something had hit him? And then a kind of a shout. I don't know whether it was Dr. Watson or not. I couldn't recognise the voice. I said, 'Doctor Watson? Doctor Watson, are you there?' But there wasn't any answer, and then someone on the other end of the line must have hung up the telephone."

Becky stopped speaking and drew an uneven breath, her eyes still brimming. "Something must have happened to him to make him stop talking to me like that. Something bad."

I was inclined to believe that Becky was right, but I didn't want to say as much out loud. Instead, I put my arm around her. "Listen, Becky, whatever happened to interrupt Watson— whoever tried to attack him, if it was an attack—Watson must have escaped. He must have, otherwise they wouldn't have bothered with releasing his photograph to the papers and starting everyone, police included, hunting for him. I don't know exactly what their objective is, but by calling down a manhunt on him, they're trying to slow him down or stop him from accomplishing ... something. Maybe to do with whatever he learned about their organisation while he was taken captive? Maybe he somehow found out their plans and was trying to get word to Holmes so that he could thwart them."

The telephone rang again in the hall below.

I took the stairs two at a time, with Becky clattering behind me, then snatched up the receiver.

"Hello?"

8. WATSON

The cab stopped for a few moments beneath the towering arched facade of Victoria Station, where a crowd of people had temporarily blocked our progress. Idly I watched them, getting in and out of carriages, calling for baggage-handlers, one person hardly distinguishable from the next.

But perhaps twenty yards away from where we stopped there stood a woman dressed in white. My gaze fastened onto her, as if magnetically attracted.

She wore a wide-brimmed white hat and her white dress shone brilliantly in the sun. She held a white parasol. Even from that distance I could see she was sharp-featured, dark-haired, and proud. She was not the only woman so dressed, for this was the summer, and white was fashionable, and so were parasols.

But my gaze picked her out from the crowd and would not let go.

Speak of the devil, I thought.

Probably because I had been thinking about her only moments before. I recognised her. And I drew in my breath.

Mrs. Torrance.

Sonnebourne's words came back to me.

Before you leave Constantinople, shoot the Torrance woman as well. She is working for Holmes.

"Hold up, Cabbie," I said. I got out. Took a five-pound note from my pocket. Turned my gaze back to see Mrs. Torrance.

A uniformed attendant was loading her luggage onto a cart. Clearly, she was preparing to board a train.

And if she was to be in Constantinople, where the assassin had been ordered to kill her, she would be taking the train to Dover.

And if she was working for Holmes ...

And Holmes was not at Baker Street ...

I tried to think clearly. But fatigue and lack of nourishment still addled me. The same questions circled through my mind.

Would Holmes also be going to Constantinople? He might very well be, if Mrs. Torrance was going there.

But if the alliance was a secret one, why would Holmes risk being seen with her?

"Sir?" came the voice of the cabbie. "Waiting will be extra."

I made up my mind. My plans seemed to fall into place. I would write out two telegraph messages and send them to both Holmes at Baker Street and Mycroft at The Diogenes Club. Then I would look for Holmes in Victoria Station. If I found him, all would be resolved. If not, I would board the Dover train. If I only saw Mrs. Torrance, I would confront her. If I were satisfied that she really was working for Holmes, I would warn her.

And upon reaching Dover, I would find a place to sleep and take some proper nourishment.

I paid the cab driver. I found the telegraph office and sent my two messages. Then, in a secluded corner of the station, I left my borrowed policeman's uniform coat and helmet. I boarded the Dover train just as it was pulling out, paid the conductor for my second-class ticket, and settled into my seat at the back of the carriage.

I shut my eyes. *Only for a moment*, I told myself.

9. LUCY

I had been praying that I would hear Watson's voice on the line. Or Jack, telephoning to tell me that Watson was safe and unharmed. But instead, a man's breathy, slightly adenoidal voice answered me.

"Is that 221B Baker Street?"

"Yes, it is."

"Residence of Mr. Sherlock Holmes?" The speaker brought the words out with a slow deliberation.

"That's right."

"Well, now." Having settled matters to his satisfaction, the speaker went on with the same ponderously slow manner. "This is Constable Oakes of the Dartford Police Station. A Mr. Mycroft Holmes left word with the Inspector here that Mr. Sherlock Holmes was to be kept informed, and so the Inspector asked me to telephone to you—"

"Informed of what?"

"There's been a body found."

My heart stopped for a moment, thinking of Watson, then restarted as the pieces belatedly clicked together in my mind. The village of Dartford was only about three miles away from the Harwell estate; I had seen it on the map this morning.

"A body? Do you mean Lord Harwell?"

"Well, it does look as though that's the way of it." I could imagine Constable Oakes on the other end of the line giving a slow, judicious nod, accompanied by his audibly drawn breath. "Turned up in an irrigation ditch, he did, and clear from the start it weren't no tramp. Dressed in a rich man's clothes and carrying a gold seal on his watch chain. That's how we discovered it was Lord Harwell, because of the family crest on the seal."

"So the body has been definitively identified, then?"

"Not for certain. That's where the Inspector's gone, to visit Harwell House and see whether he can bring Lord Harwell's poor lady to the station so she can tell us for certain that it's her husband."

I felt another twinge of sympathy for Lady Harwell. Nothing about her life had likely prepared her for the harsh realities she was about to face.

"Do you know the cause of death?"

"Not as yet." Constable Oakes breathed heavily again, then said, "Our police surgeon couldn't be sure, not without an autopsy. Said it might be heart failure. Or a stroke."

Heart failure didn't fit at all with Mycroft's suspicions of Lord Harwell's having been killed for the sake of the state secrets he possessed. But then, if Lord Harwell had been poisoned, there wouldn't be obvious signs of it.

"I see. Well, thank you for letting us know, and I'll see that Mr. Holmes gets the message."

Although Holmes, like me, would find himself hard-pressed to care about the details surrounding Lord Harwell's death when our fears for Watson were so much more overwhelming.

Becky had been listening with wide eyes and barely-concealed impatience while I talked, and burst out as soon as I'd hung up the telephone, "Well? Is there any word about Doctor Watson? I could tell it wasn't his voice on the line, but

I couldn't hear what the man was saying."

"No, I'm sorry—"

Before I could finish, the front door crashed open with enough force to rattle the front windows, and Holmes burst in like a tornado in tall, gaunt human form.

"Maps! I need a large-scale map of Clapham, ordinance surveys, and the results of the most recent government census." His eyes had the abstracted look that meant that eighty percent of his attention was focused on whatever theory he was currently developing, and that Becky and I could either help or stand out of his way.

"Clapham?"

"The Lavender Hill police station where Watson was arrested is near Clapham Common." Holmes, already halfway up the stairs, tossed the words back at me over his shoulder. "The police officers there appear to be lacking in basic intelligence to an almost super-human degree. But they were able to tell me that Watson was discovered unconscious, in the company of his two supposed murder victims ..."

Holmes seized hold of his stack of London maps, scattering several across the floor in the process, jerked open the one dealing with Clapham, scanned it, and then stabbed with his finger at a small curved road labelled *Meteor Street*. "Here. One assumes that his kidnappers had the rudimentary good sense not to leave him directly outside their front door."

Holmes swept an arm across the breakfast table, clearing off in a single avalanche the morning papers, several books, and a teacup which I narrowly rescued from smashing on the floor. He spread out the map on the newly cleared surface and bent to study it, still speaking.

"However, transporting both an unconscious man and a dead body through the streets of London is an undertaking fraught with potential complications. One would imagine that they would not have taken him far—say, no more than a mile or two at most—from the house in which he was being held. There is a chance—and I admit that it is only a chance—"

He stopped as Becky appeared beside him with a thick manila file in her hands.

"What's this?"

"All of Mycroft's reports about people associated with the Sons of Helios. Their names and addresses and everything." Becky handed Holmes the file. "That's what you're going to do, isn't it? Check through and see whether anyone associated with the Helios people owns any properties in or near Clapham?"

Holmes stared at her a moment, then the grimness that etched his features relaxed in a brief smile. "As you say. After a morning spent communing with the imbeciles in charge of the Clapham Police, it is a relief to meet with an intelligent mind at last."

"You need to hear what else Becky has to tell you," I said. "Watson was able to telephone here earlier, while we were gone."

Holmes listened with focused attention while Becky relayed her account of Watson's telephone call again.

"That confirms beyond doubt that the account I received at the Lavender Hill police station was falsified," he said when she had finished. "They would have me believe that Watson attacked a police constable in order to make his escape. They also said Watson was bearing papers that identified him as Lord Harwell."

"Who has vanished."

"Perhaps the kidnappers intended to kill Watson and have

the body discovered and identified as Lord Harwell's."

"But now that he has escaped, they must change their plan."

"It also sounds as though at least some of the constabulary at Lavender Hill may be in the pay of Lord Sonnebourne and the rest of his organisation, which isn't good news for the cause of seeing justice done. But it does make it more likely that they have some sort of headquarters in that area—otherwise why bribe the local constabulary?"

"Why indeed?" Holmes opened the file Becky had handed him and began to rifle through, tossing each paper to the floor as he finished with it. Mrs. Hudson was going to have an aneurism when she saw what Holmes had done to the room—or she would have, if she weren't too worried over Watson to care.

Holmes's brows were still knitted, even as he scanned rapidly through the list of names.

"There's nothing else that you can recall?" he asked Becky. "You heard Watson say that it was vitally important that he convey what he had learned about the 'Or—' and then he must have been forced to drop the phone. You heard nothing, however faint, that might indicate how he meant to finish that message?"

Becky shook her head. "No. I'm sorry! I wish I had!"

"It can't be helped. You did well to remember the rest of the conversation exactly." I could almost see the blend of tension and frustration that ran through Holmes like an electric current under the skin. But he spoke with what was for him uncharacteristic gentleness. "We must simply hope that we find—ah!" He broke off, seizing hold of one of the file sheets hard enough to crinkle the paper's edges.

"You've found something?" I asked.

"Adam North." Holmes read from the paper, a rising note

of grim triumph in his tone. "Known associate of Lord Son-nebourne and the Sons of Helios, according to Mycroft. In possession of a number of properties in and around London, one of them being a house on Gowrie Road, in Clapham."

10. LUCY

"So Lord Harwell's body has been found near to his estate," Holmes said. "When?"

"This morning, when Watson was being held in the Lavender Hill station," I said.

"Thankfully, that rules out the possibility that the body is Watson's."

We were in a hansom cab, rattling our way through the five-mile journey that would take us across Vauxhall Bridge and finally to Clapham. I had used the journey so far to bring Holmes up to date on the latest developments in the Harwell case.

"But the body was found in a farmer's irrigation ditch. And no signs of violence indicate that he died by sinister means. So it may not be Lord Harwell's. From what we learned he didn't strike me as the type to go wandering about the countryside alone."

We bounced over a rut in the cobblestones that made the carriage springs squeak and our seat sway.

"Especially with his tendency to gout," Holmes agreed. "Lord Harwell would have been far more likely to ride anywhere he wished to go in his own carriage. And with Sonnebourne and his organisation involved, the body may be a substitute. One moment." He broke off speaking and rapped on the ceiling trapdoor to attract the driver's attention. "Halt, please."

Our cabbie was a crabbed, elderly individual who seemed to regard all of London and its foibles with a rheumy and jaded eye. He had, his overall appearance said, seen every manner of oddity that the great city could offer, and now nothing would shock him.

However, when the carriage drew to a halt and Holmes and I exited, we found the driver staring in astonishment at the two small figures who had been riding along by clinging to the bar beneath the driver's seat.

Holmes regarded Becky and Flynn with no surprise whatsoever. "When stealing a ride on a hansom cab, one must take into consideration whether the individual whom you are attempting to follow is observant enough to notice the effect that your added weight at the back is having on the cab's manoeuvring. One of you might have gotten away with it. The two of you combined are enough to make your presence quite obvious, particularly when the cab drives over a bump."

His tone was mild, but Flynn got very busy studying his own shoes. Becky was the first to speak. "We're sorry. We only wanted to help find Doctor Watson!"

Holmes gave a questioning glance at me. I hadn't been aware of the carriage's altered manoeuvring from their weight. But I ought to have noticed that Becky had been far too willing to be left behind in Baker Street. I hadn't realised that Flynn had returned, but he must have arrived just as Holmes and I were leaving.

I weighed our options. "With Watson on the run, it's not very likely that they'll have left anyone at the house in Clapham, in case he gets in touch with us or Scotland Yard and is able to lead us back to it. At most, they'll have a single guard on watch outside the place, on the chance that Watson finds his way back alone and can be taken captive again."

"True," Holmes agreed. "Ours is primarily a reconnaissance gathering, in hopes that they may have left some clue that will point us towards their plans—and thus towards Watson's current location. One would have expected him to make his way back to Baker Street by now. Unless he has some far more urgent mission at hand." Holmes's brows furrowed, but he turned to Flynn and Becky. "Very well, the pair of you may stay. Both because returning you to Baker Street would take time and because I am loath to refuse any extra pairs of observant eyes in our search of the Clapham premises. Mind you!" He held up a finger as Becky started to speak. "You will both promise me here and now that you will exercise the greatest of care. No risks. No going off alone. These are ruthless and dangerous people with whom we are dealing, and underestimating them would be a grave if not mortal error."

Becky and Flynn looked somewhat awe-struck that they weren't being either punished or sent straight home. But their heads bobbed in simultaneous agreement.

"Right you are, Mr. 'Olmes."

"We promise," Becky echoed.

Holmes gave them both hard looks, but finally nodded. "In that case, I believe you will be more comfortable if you pass the remainder of the journey in the carriage seats with Lucy and me."

* * *

Adam North's house on Gowrie Road proved to be the end unit of a rather dreary row of square brick town-houses, with nothing at first glance to distinguish it from the neighbouring houses on either side. Having paid off the cabbie, Holmes stood regarding it for a moment.

Tattered and dirty curtains covered the windows, but there were no lights showing through the gaps or any other hint of occupancy from within.

"I don't see a sign of anyone watching," I murmured. I had been scanning the street. There were several women with shopping baskets over their arms, a chimney sweep, and a rat catcher with his terrier dog on a leash, all passing along the road. But no idle loungers who just happened to be parked on the pavement opposite, no one who appeared to be going about their own business, but was in fact keeping a watch on the property.

Holmes nodded and started up the short brick walkway that led up to the front door.

It had rained two days ago but been fine ever since, and now there were crumbles and patches of dried mud on the bricks. Holmes peered at them.

"Several individuals have passed this way as recently as yesterday evening. Men, wearing common labourer's boots. There are two distinct sizes. And a third man, who wore a gentleman's dress shoes and gaiters and walked with a slight limp." He bent to study the impressions in the mud more closely. "I believe I can also detect the prints of a woman—"

"If you're looking for them's as were lodging at number twelve, they've all gone." The voice, loud, female, and strident, came from a woman who had just emerged from the house next door—ostensibly to shake out her front rug, but more likely to find out what we were doing. Stout, with thin lips and keen dark eyes, she took in our appearance with a curiosity that fairly bristled from the ends of her stringy black hair.

"I see." Holmes, as quick as anyone I had ever known to take a potential witness's measure, drew out a half-crown from his pocket and held it meditatively in one hand. "That is a pity. I had heard that a friend of mine was visiting here, and had hoped to find him. But they are gone, you say?"

"Cleared out just after midnight, all of them. Saw 'em load a pile of trunks and boxes into a carriage and drive off." The woman's eyes were fixed on the half-crown, but she gave a snort of derision. "And if they're friends of yours, Guv, I can tell you I don't think much of 'em! Up and making noise at all hours of the day and night, they were. I 'ad to pound on the wall twice last night and tell 'em to pipe down so's I could get to sleep!"

"Most inconsiderate. You ought surely to be recompensed for the annoyance they caused." Holmes added a second half-crown to the first. "I wonder if you can describe any of the people you saw living here?"

The woman looked blank. "If I can wha'?"

"What he's wondering is whether his friend's wife might have come to stay here as well," I said. "I have a picture of her here."

Holmes gave me a quick glance of surprise as I drew out the photograph of Mrs. Torrence that I'd taken from his files before we left Baker Street. We had been chasing her long enough that I wasn't willing to let any opportunity to track her pass by.

"Oh, 'er." The woman nodded, eyeing the picture. "Came a day or two ago, she did. Didn't stay long, though."

"A day or two ago? That would be the sixth or seventh?" Holmes asked. I could see his quickening interest, though he kept his tone casual.

"Dunno about that." The woman shrugged.

"I see. And when everyone left? Did you notice how many people there were?"

"Three men. One of them must have been taken poorly, I think. The other two'd got 'im all wrapped up in a cloak and blankets and were carrying 'im between them. I thought maybe as 'ow they were taking 'im to a doctor. They packed 'im into the carriage, then loaded the trunks on afterwards. And mortal 'eavy one of 'em must 'ave been, because it took the two of them—big strong fellows both of 'em—to lift it."

Watson. I had no doubt that the supposedly ill man had been Uncle John.

"Did you see which way they went?"

"Dunno." The woman shrugged again.

Beyond learning that Watson and Mrs. Torrence had definitely been here, we were no nearer to finding them than before. And we had clearly reached the limit of what useful facts the neighbour woman could tell us.

"Well, we thank you kindly for taking the trouble to speak with us," Holmes said. "We'll just go and see whether my friend left any message for us as to where he might have gone."

I couldn't tell whether our informant continued to believe in the fiction of Holmes's friend or not, but she snatched the coins from his hand and waddled back in through her own front door.

Becky and Flynn were already at the house, peering in through the front windows.

"No one about," Flynn reported. "Everything's quiet as a grave."

"The front door is locked, though. Should we pick it?" Becky asked.

"Not too obviously. We don't wish to arouse undue suspicions among the neighbours. Or be forced to explain our presence here to the local police, whom we know already are not to be trusted." A furrow marked the space between Holmes's brows, and he glanced quickly up and down the street. Nothing had changed; it was the same ordinary scene of London street life as before, without anything to arouse suspicion. But Holmes's frown remained.

"Is something wrong?" I asked.

He shook his head as though to dislodge an errant thought. "Nothing definite. But I think we would be wise not to go in through the front door. The place feels too quiet, somehow."

Holmes might scoff at tales of second sight and supernatural premonition. But he also had not survived as long as he had in a dangerous profession by ignoring the subconscious awareness of danger that manifested as nothing more definite than a prickle at the back of the neck.

Either Holmes's uneasiness was catching, or else I felt it, too. There was nothing here that I could put my finger on as clearly wrong, but the cold inching its way across my skin refused to be dispelled.

Flynn had gone off to scout about the place, and now reappeared from around the side of the house, popping his head out from the narrow alley that separated this block of town homes from the next. "There's a window half open at the back," he said. "Kitchen, it looks like. I could maybe get in that way, open the door for the rest of you."

"Yes, very well, we'll have a look," Holmes said.

As Flynn had said, the window at the back opened into the kitchen, although the interior of the house was so dim and the window grimy enough that it was difficult to make out much besides the hulking outline of a big iron stove and a rickety-looking table. Afternoon shadows were beginning to fall, turning the dreary greys of the small paved yard where we stood greyer still.

Flynn tugged on the window sash, which looked half-rotten and was covered in peeling paint. "Give us a 'and 'n I'll be in in two shakes." He out of all of us didn't seem to have been affected by whatever had disturbed Holmes.

Holmes lent his own efforts to prying up the window, which resisted, stuck, then finally slid up with a screech that sounded loud enough to bring all the neighbours running. But nothing happened. The yard remained empty, save for ourselves, the house deserted and silent.

"All right, 'ere goes nothing." Flynn hoisted himself up onto the window ledge and swung a leg over the sill.

"Be careful!" Becky had been quiet but now spoke up, her voice sounding edged with worry.

"Nothing to it, see?" Unconcerned, Flynn ducked under the window's frame, swung his other leg over, and dropped down inside with a thump—and then a sharply metallic click.

"Don't move!" Holmes's voice rang out instantly, crisp and authoritative. "If you wish to remain alive, do not move one single muscle, Flynn, do you understand me?"

"What is it?" Flynn had frozen just inside the room in response to Holmes's order.

Holmes edged nearer to the window, close enough that he could peer inside. "Unless I am mistaken, there is a pressure plate secreted beneath the floorboards, linked to an explosive device that was activated when Flynn stepped upon it and that will detonate when his weight is removed."

I stared at him. "What?" We had dealt with bombs and explosives before, but I had never heard of such a thing.

"If I am correct, the device is similar to the land mines employed by the British Army during the Siege of Khartoum in 1884." Holmes spoke half absently, the majority of his attention clearly focused on a furious examination of our options.

Flynn gulped. "What if I just jump out of the way?"

"Unfortunately, no matter how fast you move, the blast of the explosive would be great enough to reach you."

"Don't move!" Becky was peering in through the window, her face gone very white as she clutched at the sill. "Don't move a single bit!"

"Oh, well, I was planning on practicing my dance steps, but now you say that—" Flynn couldn't risk turning his head to look at her, but he sounded as though he was gritting his teeth.

"Could we defuse the bomb somehow?" I asked Holmes. One of our more memorable cases had involved a timed detonator attached to several sticks of dynamite, and we had just barely managed to cut the bomb's wires in time to prevent its going off.

Holmes shook his head. "From what I can tell from the outside here, the entire apparatus is contained under the floorboards. With time, we might succeed in removing some of the neighbouring floorboards to gain access. But that effort might also cause enough vibration to trigger the detonator."

"Do you think the front door is set with an explosive like this, too?"

"I cannot be certain, but I should think it not very likely," Holmes said. "Everything points to this being the primary trap—the locked front door, the half-open window, offering a chance to get into the house surreptitiously, without attracting notice from the street."

Anger vibrated in his tone. Flynn's current position wasn't Holmes's fault, but he blamed himself nonetheless—and would a thousand times more if anything happened to Flynn today.

We needed another solution, and quickly. There was a limit to how long Flynn could hold perfectly still. Sooner or later, muscle fatigue would set in and cause him to shift weight.

Flynn cleared his throat, breaking the moment of silence. "I reckon you should get out. All of you."

"What? No!" Becky looked up at me, horrified. "We're not leaving you! Are, we, Lucy?"

"Of course not. Flynn, listen, we're going to find a way to get you out of there."

"That'd be nice. But I'm not seeing any way it's going to 'appen." Flynn's voice wavered briefly, then firmed. "I've 'ad some near shaves and pulled through. But everyone's luck's gotta run out. I reckon I'm for it this time. So go on. Scarper! There's no point in all of us getting blown to bits." He stopped, swallowing, then added, "Thanks for everything, Mr. 'Olmes. You've always been decent to me."

"Enough!" Holmes's expression could have been carved out of granite, which meant that he was more worried than he wanted any of us to believe. But he went on in the same crisp tone. "There will be no need for heroism or dramatic last speeches. What we need is a solution that will allow you to walk out of there without triggering the bomb."

"But what if there's no way out?" Flynn had been holding amazingly steady for an eleven-year-old boy, but now I could hear a thread of panic starting to creep into his tone. "I can't just stand here for hours, waiting for the moment when I 'ave to move and get blown up. I'd rather it happened quick, before

I've got time to dread it! If you all leave so's I know you'll be safe, I could just get it over with—"

"You will do nothing of the sort!" Holmes's voice rang with authority. "All the enemies we have faced together, all the criminals we have brought down have been unable to kill you—and now you seriously propose to save them the trouble by doing the job for them? Without so much as a fight?"

I still couldn't see Flynn's face, but his spine straightened, and he drew a shaky breath. "No, Mr. 'Olmes."

"That's better. Now, Flynn, how much do you weigh?"

"I don't know. Maybe five stone?"

I saw where Holmes was leading and turned to Becky. "Go and look in that shed over there." I gestured to a small outbuilding at the back of the dingy yard, of the sort usually used to store tools. "See whether there's a bucket—a sack—anything that could hold a quantity of weight. Look for a rope or a chain, too."

"What are you going to do?" Becky asked.

"Go back to the street and see whether there's a coal vendor about who will sell me about five stone weight of coal." Or rocks. I wasn't particular. If a potato seller appeared and offered me a hefty enough sack of his wares, I would welcome him with open arms.

11. LUCY

I didn't find a coal vendor, but half a block up the street I did find an elderly woman selling bags of sand, of the sort scullery maids used for scouring pots in the kitchen. She was mildly surprised but entirely incurious as to why I was asking to purchase the majority of her supply. And for a five-pound note, she happily accepted my offer to purchase her wheelbarrow for transporting the goods, as well. The last I saw, she was shuffling her way up the street, probably to regale her friends in the nearest gin hall with the story of the strange American woman who had offered her a near-fortune for a rusty wheelbarrow.

"Excellent," Holmes said, when I had returned to the rear yard with my purchases. "That should work admirably."

Becky had succeeded in unearthing a large burlap sack from the tool shed, and together we worked to fill it with sand.

"How closely do we have to match Flynn's weight?" I asked.

"Exact precision should not be necessary," Holmes said. "If we are within a margin of half a pound or so, that ought to be close enough. We should, though, err on the side of making the sack's weight heavier than Flynn. If I am correct about the bomb's mechanism, Flynn's weight is currently keeping the sensor depressed. If the weight we substitute for him is light enough to allow it to release, the explosive could be triggered."

Half a pound still seemed like far too narrow a margin of error, and there would be no second chances if we got it wrong.

We worked in silence, and then Holmes straightened, hefting the burlap sack in one arm.

"I believe that ought to do."

I resisted the impulse to ask whether he was sure; obviously he was, or he wouldn't be willing to take the risk.

Becky went to the window to look in at Flynn. A trickle of sweat was running down the back of his neck and his muscles were shaking a little; whether we'd gotten the weight right or no, he couldn't stand there holding perfectly motionless much longer.

"How are you feeling?" Becky asked him.

"Ask me again in five minutes?" Flynn turned his head a fraction, licking his lips. "What's the plan, Mr. 'Olmes?"

Holmes approached the window, weighted bag in hand. "I'm going to lower this through the window and onto the floor where you stand. At the precise moment it touches the ground, you will jump away—a distance of two or three feet should put you clear of the pressure plate."

"And if I don't jump fast enough?" Flynn asked.

"I cannot say for certain." Holmes's voice was calm, but I could hear the tension underlying the words. "But it is possible that the added pressure of double the weight on top of the bomb might cause it to explode."

The timing had to be impeccable, in other words.

"I don't think I can do this!" Flynn's voice rose. "I can't—"

"Yes, you can." Holmes cut in. "You have over the past few years of our association impressed me with your nerve and dedication, and I am notoriously difficult to impress. You can do this now."

"All right." Flynn still sounded shaky, but he gave the barest fraction of a nod.

"Very well." Holmes turned to Becky and me. "While I appreciate what you said earlier about not abandoning him, there is no reason for all of us to remain in danger now."

I nodded. "Come, Becky. We'll go and wait behind the shed." It was built of brick, and ought to be strong enough to offer protection—

I didn't want to finish that thought.

Becky held back a moment, resisting when I took her hand. "Flynn, just in case—" her voice wobbled.

"Who's giving last speeches now?" he asked.

Becky swallowed hard. "You still owe me a shilling from the other day when we wanted peppermints from the sweet shop, but you were out of money and I had to buy them for both of us. So don't die, because otherwise you'll never be able to pay me back!"

Flynn gave a smothered sound that might have been a laugh, and his voice sounded a little more back to his ordinary one when he said, "It's a bargain."

Becky held tight to my hand as we crossed to the rear of the yard and crouched down behind the tool shed. We waited. Neither of us spoke, but every second seemed to crawl by interminably. I couldn't see or hear anything from the house. Had Holmes attempted to lower the sand bag weight in yet?

But after what seemed an eternity, Holmes's voice rang out. "All clear!"

When we emerged, Holmes was standing by the window, rope in hand, and Flynn was still inside on the far end of the kitchen, looking dazed, as though he couldn't entirely believe that he was still alive and breathing.

"It worked!" I couldn't quite believe it, either.

"Indeed." Predictably, Holmes had already recovered enough that he sounded entirely unruffled. "And now I believe we ought to turn our attention to—carefully—searching the premises. It would give me great pleasure to find a clue that would allow us to confront whoever set this bomb."

* * *

The interior of the house, though, proved remarkably and disappointingly lacking in anything that might point us towards where our enemies had gone. The kitchen cupboards were bare, the fireplaces were swept entirely clean; the rooms were dusty and covered with a layer of grime, but empty of anything more than a few pieces of cheap furniture. Apparently when they had packed up and left yesterday morning with Watson in tow, they had done a thorough job.

"Nothing," Holmes growled in frustration. We had already made a preliminary sweep through the house. Now, prostrate on the ground, he was making a minute examination of the floorboards in the front room. "Not so much as a cigar ash or a broken end of a matchstick. Judging by the footmarks in the dust, our friend from outside who walks with a limp was here a day or two ago, but otherwise—"

"Wait a moment." I held up a hand, feeling as though I was hearing Holmes's observation for the first time. "A man who walks with a limp." I peered down at the dusty prints. My ability to read foot marks was nowhere near as accurate as Holmes's, but I said, "His right leg is the one with the weakness, wouldn't you say?"

"Correct." Holmes frowned, for once not seeming to leap to the same conclusion that I had done. Maybe because the idea that had suddenly struck me was so far-reaching that it could scarcely be called a conclusion at all.

"I saw a telephone cabinet out in the hall." It was one of the few articles that hadn't been removed—and proof, if we had needed it, that there was money backing the group that had lodged here. Telephones were by no means common in this part of Clapham.

A few minutes later I had succeeded in asking the operator to connect me to the Dartford Police Station, and was speaking once again to the adenoidal Constable Oakes.

"I'm speaking on behalf of Sherlock Holmes," I said, when we had finished with making our introductions. "I wanted to check on whether Lady Harwell has been in to identify her husband's body."

"Oh aye, that she has. Took on terribly at the sight of him, poor lady. Cried and came over all faint. We had to fetch a doctor who could see to her and bring her back home."

"I see." That was nothing more than I had expected. But my heart quickened as I went on, "Thank you. Now, there's just one further question I need to ask."

12. WATSON

I awoke. The train was not moving. There were no passengers in my carriage. No luggage. I looked for the conductor. Nowhere to be seen. Groggy with sleep, I stumbled out of the carriage and onto the platform.

An attendant was positioning an empty baggage cart. I walked over to him.

"Which way to the ferry?" I asked.

"Down to docks," he said, and pointed.

"Thank you." I started to walk in that direction.

"But you won't find the ferry."

"What?"

"Gone. You missed it."

"When is the next one?"

"9:40. Tomorrow morning." He gave me a strange look. "You look all in, mate," he said. "I'd get some sleep if I were you."

13. LUCY

"We are sorry to trouble you at this late hour, Lady Harwell." Holmes bent low over the lady's hand. "But we wished to express our condolences personally to you on the sad loss of your husband."

Lady Harwell was very much as we had left her that morning, reclining on the sofa in her parlour. Although she had changed her dress, and now wore heavy mourning: a bombazine gown of deep black, trimmed with jet beads that clinked together whenever she moved.

She raised a handkerchief to her eyes. That, too, was different from this morning, being edged with black ribbon. "Thank you, Mr. Holmes. As you can see, I am utterly prostrated from the shock. That such a thing can have happened to my poor Gerald! That he should leave me utterly alone in this way—" her voice broke.

"It is hard to be alone," I said. "But there are consolations, of course. For example, a wife's money belongs to her husband, even if it is hers by birthright. But a widow has control of her own fortune, to spend or save as she pleases."

Lady Harwell's small dark eyes widened for a split second. Then she shook her head, sitting up with indignation. "Why, really, I can't imagine what you mean, saying a thing like that. I assure you that money is the very last thing that matters to me at such a time as this—"

"Is it?" I leaned forward. "Your husband recently visited the dentist's, didn't he? To have a tooth extracted?"

Lady Harwell's doughy features went blank with surprise. "Why, yes. But why—"

"The man currently lying in the mortuary at the Dartford Police Station has all his teeth intact. I don't know who he is, but he's not your husband."

"I—I—" Lady Harwell's mouth opened and closed with no more sound emerging.

"It must have been difficult for you," I went on. "Watching your wastrel of a husband squander your fortune, and being powerless to stop him. Then you learned that he planned to turn traitor to his country—sell the state secrets he was in possession of, fake his own death by means of a body substitute—and escape under a new identity, provided for him by a certain criminal organisation that specialises in such fresh starts for wealthy criminals. He probably coached you in what you would have to do, once his supposed body was found—how you would have to identify him. Was that when it occurred to you that it was a perfect chance to get rid of him permanently, without a shadow of blame attaching to you? Because of course, there would be no signs of foul play on the body that would be found—and anyway, you could be proved never to have left the house here at the time when he died."

Lady Harwell's fingers were clutching the string of black beads at her neck, her face gone an odd mottled colour. "I— you're lying! All of this is a tissue of wicked lies, you can't prove any of it!"

"I think, you know, that we can." I nodded to Holmes, who drew back the curtains that covered the parlour window facing out onto the grounds. The slope of grass and trees were in darkness, save for a few specks of yellow illumination that flickered and danced across the lawn. "Do you see those lights out there, Lady Harwell? Those are police officers breaking into the icehouse. I think we both know what they're going to find there."

"I don't—you can't—"

"You killed your husband, Lady Harwell. Then very early in the morning when no one was about, you concealed his body in the ice house—likely at the back, well covered in layers of sawdust, where it would not be discovered until you had a chance to move it to some more permanent hiding place. You were seen that morning, though, by one of the gardeners, and since I am certain that it is indeed a rare occurrence for you to set foot outside this room, you had to give some account of your presence there. Hence the story of the unsatisfactory roses, and your threat to dismiss the gardener who had seen you."

Lady Harwell stared at me a moment, her eyes narrowed, her cheeks unhealthily flushed. Then her mouth twisted. The words seemed almost to burst out on their own in an angry flood. "Do you know what Gerald was like? For years he squandered my money on his drink and his gambling! Then he planned to just walk away and leave—taking as much as he could grab of my fortune with him! He laughed about it, said that he would soon be living the high life in South America without a care in the world. And he expected me to help him do it! He said there would be a scandal if it came out that he had sold state secrets, and my name would be disgraced. So to avoid it, I was to identify the false body as his." Her eyes darkened with the memory. "He laughed and said he hoped I'd give him a good funeral. It never occurred to him that I wouldn't do exactly as he said. He never even considered me a threat!" She stopped, panting for breath, and then a small smile played about the corners of her mouth. "I stabbed him straight through the heart with my letter opener. The one I keep right there, on the desk." She gestured. "And never in my life have I seen a man look so surprised."

* * *

"What will happen to her, do you think?" I asked Holmes.

We were in our carriage on the way back home. I hadn't looked out the window, but just by the familiar rattle of the cobblestones I could feel that we were nearly at Baker Street.

"Consideration may be given to her on the grounds that her husband was guilty of treason. With a good lawyer, she may escape being hanged." The glow of Holmes's lighted pipe was a small orange ember in the darkness opposite me. It moved; he must have unclamped it from between his teeth. "Why do you ask? Are you feeling sorry for her?"

"Not particularly." I had felt pity for Lady Harwell at the beginning of the case. But Holmes and I dealt with murderers on practically a daily basis—and nearly all of them tried to convince us of the righteousness of their crimes. "I was just wondering whether she might know anything that will point us towards Lord Sonnebourne. If her husband confided in her at all—"

"It is unlikely that she knows anything of value, but the question must be delved into," Holmes said. He sounded slightly weary; we were both feeling the effects of the past several days.

"I suppose that they planned for the false body found in the drainage ditch to be identified as Lord Harwell some days ago. But then when Watson escaped—and thanks to Lady Harwell,

Lord Harwell truly had disappeared—they altered their plans and decided to have Watson identified as Harwell. But I still don't entirely see what their aim was."

"That, too, must be investigated," Holmes said.

With a final rattle, our cab drew to a halt, and I looked out to see the number 221B illuminated by the carriage lamps. I was suddenly exhausted, as though a giant lump of fatigue had been dropped on me from above. Tomorrow, we would continue the search for Watson and our fight to find evidence against Lord Sonnebourne's organisation. But for right now, all I wanted was to collect Becky and go home to where Jack—

The front door of 221B opened, and Mrs. Hudson's plump form stood illuminated against the light of the front hall.

"Mr. Holmes? Is that you?" She peered out at our carriage.

"What have you, Mrs. Hudson?" Any sign of tiredness entirely gone, Holmes leaped from the cab, landing on the pavement.

"It's a telegram, Mr. Holmes. It came this afternoon."

Holmes was already ripping open the sheet in Mrs. Hudson's hands. I flung a handful of change at our driver, then scrambled out to join him, peering over his shoulder.

The message had been sent from Victoria Station, by "JHW." It contained only these words:

Enroute to Constantinople. Danger to French official and Holmes.

SUNDAY, JULY 10

14. WATSON

I spent the night in a modest hotel near the harbour. When morning came, I felt much more like myself.

But then I went down to breakfast and picked up a newspaper from a stack at the lobby front desk. My picture was on the front page.

Wanted for Murder, the headline read. The image of my wild-eyed stare looked as though I were bewildered with drink or drugs. I remembered the young police inspector at Lavender Hill asking if I knew why I had been found unconscious with two dead men.

I put down the paper immediately, turning it over to hide my picture. I recalled first being awakened by flashes in the house near Clapham Common. So those had been flashes of a photographer's camera, and all England was now seeing the results of the photographer's work.

My name was not in the headline. At least that was something to be thankful for, although, having not read the text of the article, I could not tell whether any name had been associated with that revolting image.

As inconspicuously as I could manage, I strolled out of the hotel and down to the ferry dock in the warm morning sun, pretending to be concerned with nothing more important than taking in the fresh sea air. At a vendor's stall, I bought a straw boater hat. I tilted it at what I hoped was a rakish angle, enough to conceal part of my face. Then I boarded the ferry, taking a seat at the far end. I wanted to be one of the first to debark when we landed at Calais Harbour. In France, I reasoned, there would not be such a hue and cry for an English criminal.

Luck proved to be with me that morning, for no one accosted or questioned me during the ferry journey or on the train from Calais to Paris. I rode unchallenged all the way to the Garde Nord Station.

I took the time to plan my next move.

The most important thing was to keep Holmes informed of my whereabouts. I had with me several blank telegraph forms, taken from Victoria Station. I would write two more messages, again to Holmes at Baker Street and to Mycroft at the Diogenes Club. If Holmes had already departed, Mycroft would know how to reach him.

But what to tell them?

What had I not told them? I thought.

Then I wrote.

Continuing to Constantinople. Sonnebourne assassin has connection with Pera Palace.

I folded the two messages into two one-hundred-franc banknotes and tucked them into my right waistcoat pocket.

At the Garde Nord station, I got off the train with the other passengers. Smoke from the trains swirled throughout the crowded walkway. I was glad of it. Eyes down, squinting against the choking dust, I made my way forward, trying to remain inconspicuous.

I saw the telegraph booth at the centre of the station rotunda. But I stopped abruptly.

Waiting at the booth, his long arms dangling at his sides, was Clegg.

I hung back, letting the crowd flow past me, keeping to the other side of the booth. Then I moved over to where a shoe-shine boy sat waiting for customers. I took a fifty-franc banknote from my waistcoat pocket.

The boy became very attentive.

I have a rudimentary grasp of French, and I was able to make the boy understand what I wanted, which was for him to walk over to the telegraph booth, sit down a short distance away so as to interfere with the movement of passers-by, and not move for five minutes.

To my surprise, he replied in English, "So I don't move, whatever happens?"

I nodded, gave him the banknote, and waited until he took position. A crowd quickly gathered.

Soon Clegg stepped away from the booth to see the cause of the gathering. I eased my way into the vacated space, caught the eye of the telegraph clerk, and slid my message and the two banknotes beneath the metal grill onto the counter.

The clerk picked them up, glanced at the message, and nodded.

I mimed "hush" with my pursed lips and forefinger.

He nodded again.

I kept moving. Not looking back, trusting that the clerk would accommodate me, and hoping Clegg would not notice. Or that if he did, he would have no influence over the clerk.

My next task was to reach the eastern station, some distance away from Garde Nord, where I could board the Constantinople train. I saw a sign for an exit. I made my way along the crowded corridor and emerged into a less-crowded open area, with perhaps a half-dozen doors, already opened, along the far wall.

I felt a hand on my shoulder, and heard a familiar, ugly voice. "Where do you think you're going?"

Clegg.

Was there someone with him?

In for a penny, I thought, and motioned that the two of us should go towards the ticket wall, away from the crowd. I led him there, turned to face him, and drove my knee into his groin, taking him by surprise. He doubled over. I grabbed his collar and, rocking back, pulled him towards me, driving my knee upwards once again, connecting with his chin. Not a soul attempted to stop us. With the flow of the crowd moving towards the exit doors, it is possible that no one even noticed.

I pushed Clegg aside and left him slumped against the wall.

Outside the station, I hailed the first waiting cab. "Gare de l' Est. Wagons-Lits," I said. The driver nodded and flicked a whip over his horse.

I had the vague recollection that I would need a passport for the train to Constantinople and wished I had thought of that before sending my wire to Mycroft. But there was another way, I thought. I would take the train at least as far as Munich, where I knew a British embassy was located. I would send yet another wire to Mycroft. Possibly he could arrange matters. Even better, perhaps Mycroft could clear my name.

I entered the eastern station and hurried to the Wagons-Lits platform, arriving only a few moments before the waiting Orient Express was about to leave. One uniformed attendant stood on the otherwise empty platform. On the train behind him, the door of the last carriage remained open. I had a hundred-franc note ready for him. I held it out like a ticket and pressed it into the hand of the attendant.

"Munich," I said.

He held the note, but he frowned. "These carriages require a reservation. They are first and second class. Third class is—"

Behind me I heard an all-too familiar voice, Cockney accented, loud, and angry. "Not so fast!" I turned and saw Clegg running towards me.

Then from above me came a woman's voice. "Lord Harwell!" I looked up.

In the open railway carriage doorway stood Mrs. Torrance. She was now dressed in black silk rather than white, but her sharp features and piercing dark eyes were unmistakable as she addressed the uniformed attendant.

"He has a reservation," she said. "Harwell. Check your list."

The attendant consulted his book, nodded, and pocketed my note.

Clegg, his meaty face bruised and swollen due to our altercation, now stood beside me. He radiated heat and sweaty odour. I felt his sour breath in my face, and his thick hand grasping my upper arm.

To my astonishment, Mrs. Torrance said, "Clegg. Go back to London. Those are orders." She tossed a thick white envelope down to him. He released my arm in order to catch the envelope.

He glanced at the contents and nodded again. Then, with a sullen glare at me, he turned and walked away.

Two policemen were approaching, but Clegg passed them without stopping.

Mrs. Torrance said, "Get in." She beckoned impatiently. "Or do you want to stand on the platform and be arrested?"

I clambered up the metal steps and into the carriage. Mrs. Torrance stepped aside to let me pass. Ahead of me was an open door leading to a private sleeping compartment. I went inside and she followed. The compartment was neat and smelled of perfume. Jasmine, I thought. Faint yellow light from a small electric bulb shone on the varnished wood surfaces of the wardrobe and drawers. Those were all tightly shut. A bright blue folded silk robe occupied the far end of a narrow sofa.

She shut the door to the compartment behind her. "Mr. Holmes told me to protect you, Dr. Watson," she said.

"Clegg obeyed you," I said.

"He takes orders from those he believes are in command." She smiled, as though pleased to be sharing her secret. "Today, he believed that his commander was me. And he wanted the money in that envelope."

Was this true? Sonnebourne's words came back to my memory. *Shoot the Torrance Woman as well. She is working for Holmes.*

But Sonnebourne had given those orders to the dark-haired assassin, in the interview room that I had seen through the decoy portrait. Clegg had not been in the interview room. In fact, Clegg had been ordered to stay away.

So, yes, it was likely that Clegg did not know that Mrs. Torrance was marked for death and no longer in a position to give orders.

Ought I to warn Mrs. Torrance?

She continued, "Clegg will kill you if he can."

"When did you talk with Mr. Holmes?"

"We can go over all that later. I shall be in the dining car at seven. For now, you must go to your own compartment. You'll find clothes and your passport. Or the conductor may have it."

"Passport?"

"In a leather folder, personalised with your name. Don't lose it. You won't get to Constantinople without one. Nor even into Bulgaria, for that matter." She opened the door. "The compartment is in the next car down, on your left. Number 7."

"Did Holmes give you my passport?"

She shook her head. "The passport is in the name of Gerald, Lord Harwell. He is a client of Sonnebourne's." She paused. "He is also a Duke. So, in the dining car, you should behave like a nobleman. People on this train will expect that." She paused. "When someone says 'your grace,' or 'Lord Harwell,' don't ignore them. Milord."

I ought to be able to respond to Milord, I supposed. "Perhaps you can explain why the clothes I am wearing now have Harwell's initials," I said. "There were also tradesmen's letters—"

She cut me off. "Your body was to be discovered in London and identified as Harwell's. When you escaped, they found another substitute. The real Harwell was to travel to Constantinople on this train, and then vanish with a new identity. But since he's not here, we can use his belongings to get you out of trouble."

"Trouble?"

"Don't pretend, Dr. Watson. I saw those policemen in Paris, and I saw your picture in the newspapers before I left Dover. Now go to your compartment. Before the attendant comes."

15. LUCY

"Are you really all right about my going?" I asked.

Jack and I were sitting side by side in the familiar surroundings of 221B Baker Street. Everything from the shag tobacco kept in its slipper by the mantle to the Queen's initials VR outlined in bullets on the wall spoke of Sherlock Holmes. But it all felt somehow slightly empty, almost eerie tonight, with Holmes not here, and without any promise of when—or even if—he would return.

For answer, Jack turned to face me. The fire in the grate patched his lean face with alternate light and shadow. "Do you mind when I'm called out to a murder scene or to hunt down a violent suspect in the middle of the night?"

As an officer of Scotland Yard, he frequently was. "Well, I don't love it, but that's your job."

"There you are then."

I could tell from the quality of Jack's brief smile that it wasn't quite as simple as that. I was walking—deliberately walking—straight into a known danger, and for almost the first time since we'd met, I would be on my own.

Before I could say anything more, though, the clock on the mantle struck eleven, and Becky startled up from where she'd been dozing in an armchair by the fire. Not that she would have admitted to being asleep. At eleven years old, she considered herself far too close to adulthood to be shackled with childish constraints like bed-time.

"Is it time for you to leave, Lucy?" she asked.

"Very nearly." I got up, too, and picked up the small carpet bag I'd already packed with everything I would need.

Becky bit her lip. "Thank you for letting me stay up to say goodbye."

"I had to." I gave her a hug. "Otherwise I would have been continually checking to make sure you hadn't stowed away in my suitcase." I spoke lightly, but with her that was distinctly within the realm of possibility.

Becky didn't smile, though. "What if Dr. Watson didn't travel by the Orient Express after all?"

I sat back down on the edge of the sofa. I did need to be on my way, but Becky needed reassurance more.

"We're as sure as we can possibly be," I told her. "His telegram yesterday said that he was enroute to Constantinople. And when he spoke to you on the telephone, it sounded as though he started to say 'Orient' before he was cut off."

"He wasn't on the passenger list of the last train to depart, though," Becky said.

"No. But Lord Harwell was." Mycroft's first act after the receipt of Watson's telegram had been to demand a list of passengers from the Wagons-Lits railway company, and it had been brought by special messenger to us within the hour. One of those instances where Mycroft's high-up position within the British government was a distinct advantage. "We know that Watson was identified as Lord Harwell at the Lavender Hill Police Station. And we know that the real Lord Harwell is dead."

Holmes and I had in fact just unmasked his murderer.

"So it's likely that Watson is still travelling under Lord Harwell's identity."

Becky didn't look even slightly reassured. "Dr. Watson's telegram also said there was danger to Mr. Holmes in Constantinople."

"I know."

Those were the only two definite scraps of information that Watson had been able to impart in his maddeningly brief telegram: *Enroute to Constantinople. Danger to French official and Holmes.*

"That's why Lucy's going," Jack said quietly. "So that Mr. Holmes will have someone to watch his back."

None of us mentioned the possibility of Holmes not going to Constantinople as a result of Watson's warning. That would never be entertained as an option by anyone who knew Holmes. If anything, the direct personal threat was more along the lines of waving a red flag in front of a bull—or would be, if those animals could actually see in colour. No force on earth could have prevented Holmes from journeying to Constantinople now.

"We don't know whether Watson is acting of his own free will or whether he's being held prisoner by someone travelling with him," I said to Becky.

Something was most definitely wrong, otherwise Watson would have written to explain matters more fully. But without knowing the truth of the dangers he might be facing, we didn't dare send any telegrams in response to his. If Watson was a captive, and our enemies learned that he had succeeded in warning us, it could cost him his life.

"That's why we need to travel to Constantinople in person," I said. "Both for Watson's sake, and for the sake of whatever international disaster he's trying to prevent."

Mycroft had already booked passage for us on the Orient Express that would leave Calais the day after tomorrow. The tickets were under assumed names, and by prearranged agreement, Holmes and I would have no contact with one another from now on.

That was why Holmes was not here now: he had already departed for one of his famous bolt-holes, the rented rooms he kept all around London, stocked with everything he would need to disguise himself for the journey.

"I know." The corners of Becky's mouth were still turned down. "I just wish that I could go with you."

"Come on, Beck." Jack put an arm around his sister. "If you were gone, who'd keep an eye on me and make sure I don't get into any trouble while Lucy's away?"

Becky mustered up a wan smile, and Jack looked up at the clock. "Lucy'd better be off now."

"Is our friend the watcher in place?" I asked.

For the last two days, 221 Baker Street had been under surveillance by a wide array of individuals, from young men offering to shine boots, to flower sellers and idle loafers who mysteriously seemed to find the house across the road from ours the most comfortable building in all of London against which to lean.

Unfortunately, confronting any of them would be a waste of time. They were simple hirelings, probably with only a vague notion of their purpose in keeping watch on us.

We needed the individual closer to the top, the one giving the orders.

Jack was already standing by the window. He edged the curtain a fraction of an inch out of the way, looked out and then nodded.

"Present and correct. It's a new one, anyway. An old man slumped on the pavement and swilling something out of a bottle and pretending to be drunk. But he's keeping a sharp eye on our doorway here."

"Well, I must put on a good show for him, then." I took up my hat and coat.

"Goodbye." Becky hugged me fiercely. She didn't protest any more, or cry at my leaving. But my last sight as I reached the street and gave a final look back at the house was of her small, forlorn figure outlined in the glow of the upstairs window.

She raised her hand to wave, and I blew her a kiss. Then I turned away.

Across the road, the drunken old man heaved himself to his feet with a fairly convincing show of simply stretching his legs. Then making another show of finding his bottle empty, he shuffled after me as I walked down the road.

* * *

I was wearing my own clothes: a grey walking suit trimmed with black braid, and a matching hat. I also wore a black evening cloak around my shoulders, which in the mid-July weather was entirely unnecessary for warmth, but which did make it easier to blend into the deepest shadows at the side of the street.

I walked until I reached Park Road, where I hailed a cab. I risked a quick glance behind me. My friend the elderly reprobate was still shuffling after me, with more purpose in his steps, now. I'd walked too quickly for him to keep up the drunken act.

"St. Paul's Cathedral, please," I told the driver.

Then I climbed into the cab and settled back against the worn leather seats.

By the time we had reached our destination and I alighted before the wide stone steps, my cloak and hat had both been stuffed into my bag. I now wore a distinctly more eye-catching hat of emerald silk with a spray of ostrich feathers on one side, and a capelet of matching deep green emerald.

Inside, the sanctuary was a long, dimly lit space, with candles glowing on the altar. The faint ambient light of the outside street lamps filtered through high gothic-style stained glass windows. I wasn't the only one to seek refuge here tonight: a few shabby-looking figures were spaced out among the dark wooden pews. From the snores coming from several of them, they were less interested in worship than in finding a safe place to sleep. But then, considering my own purposes in being here, I was scarcely in a position to judge.

I knelt down in an empty pew close to the door that led back out into the knave and waited. The candles on the altar flickered. The snoring continued to echo in the vaulted space. But no one else entered behind me.

I bent my head—sincerely; I couldn't recall God owing me any favours, but I would be happy for any divine assistance offered to me tonight. Then I slowly sank down until I was crouched on the floor between the high-backed wooden pews and invisible except to anyone who looked in on me directly.

I took out my hairpins and once again opened my bag.

From there, if anyone was watching—and I distinctly hoped that they were, otherwise this night was going to be counted as a great deal of wasted effort—a bent, elderly woman with untidy grey hair and a tattered shawl exited the church. She limped her way arthritically down the road until she reached a coffee house still open at this hour of the night and entered.

There the elderly crone disappeared, to be replaced by a young, blond-haired woman in a nurse's uniform, who made her way efficiently down the street but with a slightly tired lag in her step. Anyone seeing her would assume that she was travelling home from attending a difficult medical case or a childbirth.

The nurse hailed a passing cab, which deposited her outside of a butcher's shop where Holmes had one of his famous bolt-holes in the upstairs rooms. Jack and I had taken refuge there once, before we were married. I pushed the memories away as I changed out of the nurse's uniform and into the apparel of a young man: trousers, scruffy checked coat, and a flat-brimmed hat pulled down low over my eyes. I needed all my attention focused on the job at hand tonight, not lost in the past. Although I wished that Jack were here in the room with me now.

Dressed in my boy's apparel, I exited the bolt-hole through the upper-story window, climbing down the water pipe and landing in the narrow alley that ran along the back of the butcher's shop.

At the end of the alleyway, I performed a quick scan of the road. Several pedestrians, three newspaper boys, and a few early-morning women shoppers with baskets over their arms. I had at any rate lost the old man who had been watching Baker Street; I'd not seen a sign of him since St. Paul's Church.

Hands in my pockets, I sauntered casually out of the alley and down the road, heading for Belgravia and Victoria Station.

16. WATSON

I left Mrs. Torrance in her compartment, walked down the passageway to the next railway carriage, and pushed open the heavy connecting door.

Immediately I recoiled from a blast of hot, dusty air. The roar of the locomotive and the clatter of the wheels assaulted my ears. I caught the sharp scent of lignite. My eyes stung. Beneath me, the gap between the swaying carriages closed and then widened. The bright steel rails, crushed stones, and wooden sleeper ties below me all flew past at a dizzying rate.

I had to keep moving. I pulled open the door to the next carriage and hauled myself inside. Behind me, the door clicked shut. Inside, in the relative calm, I caught my breath before I manoeuvred into the passageway. I needed to find my own compartment and get away from the public view. My face adorned the front page of newspapers both in England and in France. Thanks to the manipulations of Lord Sonnebourne and his shadowy organisation of criminals, I was a fugitive wanted for a double murder.

I stood for a moment. Outside, the French countryside floated by on my right, green fields and greener forests, visible through the large windows along the narrow corridor. On my left, I saw a row of polished wood compartment doors, identical to those in the carriage from which I had entered the train. All were securely shut. No rattling. Brass hardware locks and recessed brass handles gleamed as if brand-new.

At the end of the passageway sat a uniformed railway conductor. He was aware of my entry into his carriage, but as yet he was content merely to observe the intrusion.

I had taken many railway journeys, but never on a train so luxurious as the Orient Express. And never, I reflected, in the identity of someone else. John H. Watson, M.D., was not accustomed to travel in such circles, where the cost of train fare to my destination was a greater sum than most of my patients earned in half a year. But here, I reminded myself, I was not John H. Watson, M.D. I was impersonating a duke.

Compartment Number Seven, Mrs. Torrance had said. There I would find clothes and a false passport. I would dress for dinner and join her in the first-class dining car, where she would explain why she, a murderer Sherlock Holmes and I had been pursuing for nearly half a year, was now his ally—and also mine, since she had prevented my capture.

On the second compartment to my left, the number seven gleamed in polished brass. I tried the door. It was locked. The uniformed conductor stood up from his seat and came forward, a middle-aged man of swarthy Mediterranean features and quiet dignity. He wore a black cap and black uniform, each smartly trimmed with elegant gold braid. He held a black leather notebook in one hand. His small dark eyes met mine, respectful but with authority.

"I am Maurice, senior conductor for this sleeping car. You are, sir?"

To my chagrin, in my fatigue I momentarily forgot the name of the duke I was impersonating.

"I am on your list," I said, "to occupy Number Seven. The attendant on the platform permitted me to board."

"Noted, Sir. However, you will understand it is for your security that I must ask again for your name."

I remembered the initials in my jacket lining. I had seen them. What were they? Would I have to remove my jacket?

Then, thankfully, I remembered.

"Harwell. Gerald," I said. "I am a duke. From England. Kent."

He looked dubiously at me, and then at the paper in his leather-bound notebook.

"Yes, Milord. I have it here on my list. Number Seven. I have your passport as well."

"In your notebook?"

"I have your passport locked in my storage compartment with those of the other passengers in this carriage. I keep them there so I can show them to border officials when we cross at Strasbourg. That way, none of you need interrupt your sleep." He smiled. "You can rest undisturbed as we enter, or at any other crossing."

"I should like to see my passport. To verify that it is correct."

"Momentarily, Milord."

He produced a brass key, unlocked the compartment door, and then placed the key into my hand. He stood discreetly aside to give me an unobstructed view. A sofa on my right. Wooden cabinets on my left. And doors. All tightly shut. A small wash-stand in the corner. A mirror. A window with the shade drawn. Shelves with bottles of pomade and cologne, brushes, and shaving kit.

"The company has replaced all the sleeping cars in the fleet."

"That explains why everything looks so new. Because it is."

"Yes, Milord. I mention it because you are no doubt accustomed to the old design, since you have travelled with us before. The new design places one washroom between every pair of two compartments, rather than at the ends." He pointed along the corridor to another door, two doors down from mine. "That is the men's washroom for this carriage. Do not use the other. There are ladies travelling on the train."

I smiled. "I am meeting a lady for supper this evening."

"The first-class dining carriage is two cars further down. After the ladies' salon. Next comes the men's smoking lounge and library." He gave a brief nod. "I shall have your bed made up by the senior attendant while you are in the dining car. His name is Anthony, and he has already unpacked your suitcase. I am sure you will find all to your satisfaction. If not, would you kindly inform me, and I shall see to it personally. Now, I shall retrieve your passport."

He departed, closing the door behind him.

I inspected the clothes that hung in the wardrobe. Three jackets, one for evening wear, with matching trousers, all freshly pressed. Black silk pyjamas. Starched white collars, shirts, black silk socks, silk underwear. Three pairs of highly polished shoes, including one pair in glossy patent leather.

I touched the soft, smooth fabric of the dinner jacket. A far cry from the quality of my own wardrobe. On impulse, I looked inside the jacket lapel. The same initials, in the same gold thread: "GH." A saying of Thoreau, the American philosopher Lucy frequently quoted, came to mind: "Beware of all enterprises that require new clothes."

I wondered if any of these new clothes would fit me.

I sat on the sofa, slipped off my dusty brogan shoe and tried the patent leather. It did fit.

There came a knock at the door.

"Your passport, Milord."

Maurice handed me a flat folder of black leather, with a name printed on a strip of white satin fabric sewn onto the top: LORD HARWELL OF KENT. The folder opened to reveal a single sheet of heavy parchment, framed by the leather. The British Lion and Unicorn at the top of the parchment were the same as on my own, as was the instruction from the Prime Minister to "request and require" safe passage of the bearer wherever the passport was presented. But while after "John H. Watson" on my passport came the words "a British subject," on this one after "Gerald, Lord Harwell," were the words, "Duke of Harwell, in the County of Kent." I recalled the pride I had felt when carefully signing my name to my own passport. The signature on this one was a scrawled "Harwell." The careless indifference of Harwell's writing made me think how far from my own natural state was the role I was now playing.

"All in order, Milord?" He was setting a ceramic pitcher on the washstand.

"Thank you." I folded the binder and handed it back. Absurdly, I wondered what Holmes's passport signature looked like. His disdain for bureaucratic regulation might have elicited a scrawl just as careless as Harwell's. Particularly if he were playing the part of a contemptuous duke.

If I was to help Holmes, I needed to set aside my own misgivings and play that role.

"How long until we reach Constantinople?" I asked.

"From Paris it is normally two and one-half days. Early Wednesday morning is our scheduled arrival. Sixty-three hours." Maurice consulted his watch. "Barring unforeseen delays, naturally. There is a timetable in the drawer of your writing desk."

"How long until Munich?"

"After midnight tonight. Or possibly later."

"I shall be asleep, no doubt. Can you send a telegraph message for me?"

"From Munich?"

I nodded. "To London." I drew from my pocket my supply of paper currency and handed him two hundred-franc notes. "I shall have the message ready after supper this evening. It will be brief."

Maurice pocketed the notes and glanced over to the mirror and corner washstand. "First-class dinner service begins at seven, Milord. Please ring for me if the shaving kit or anything else does not meet with your approval. The water in the pitcher is hot." Then he gave a slight bow and departed.

I sat down heavily on the sofa, suddenly fatigued. But a glance at my pocket watch told me I would need to shave now and dress for dinner if I was to be punctual. The shaving kit contained everything I required. I stared critically at my reflection. For a fleeting moment I considered beginning a new moustache to restore what my kidnappers had taken from me, but I knew this was not the time. I was Harwell and had to look the part. I turned to my luxurious clothes. The dove-grey silk vest, the Egyptian cotton wing-tipped shirt, the velvet trimmed dinner jacket, all felt far sleeker and finer than those I wore in London. But they all fit perfectly.

I checked my reflection in the class. I thought I looked the perfect aristocrat, down to the tight symmetrical knot of my black silk tie. My fatigue had vanished.

But cold suspicion had replaced it. I determined to have an explanation from the woman who called herself Mrs. Torrance.

17. WATSON

The dining car windows were large and tall. From the small table where I sat, the green fields and hills of the French countryside seemed to race towards us, and then away. Trees and houses made long shadows that stretched out in the light of the setting sun. Across from me sat Mrs. Torrance. Her face shone with the sunlight. She drew the shade down to keep the glare from her eyes.

"The clothes in my wardrobe are a perfect fit," I said.

"You make that sound like an accusation," She tapped ash into a small silver tray, delicately grasping her long cigarette holder between her fingertips. "You men have smoking jackets to keep the ash away," she said. "Someday these will be fashionable for women."

She looked outside for a moment, ignoring the few grey flakes of ash that fell onto the white linen tablecloth. She gave a pouting smile. "Why would you complain that your wardrobe is too perfect? I thought you would enjoy a taste of luxury, Milord."

"I find it disconcerting that everything fits so well. Even the trousers, with the right leg one-quarter inch shorter than the left, to compensate for a wound I received at Kandahar. Why are the measurements of Harwell's garments all identical to mine?"

She gave me a sharp look. "You really don't understand?"

"You duplicated my entire wardrobe?"

"What you found in your compartment we had made to measure, based on your tailor's own specifications."

"When?"

"In late June. The plan has been in the works for more than a month, ever since your Mr. Holmes took that very valuable painting from Lord Sonnebourne—"

"The painting that Sonnebourne's client had stolen to pay Sonnebourne for his new identity," I said.

She gave a cold smile. "Sonnebourne considered that an affront, nonetheless, and requiring a response that would be painful to Holmes."

"Kidnapping me."

"Killing you, actually. As I said, your body was to be discovered and identified as Lord Harwell's. No such identification would survive if the measurements of the clothes on your body were not the same as those in Lord Harwell's own closet. And, given his status and wealth, such a comparison would have been made, I assure you."

"Who made the clothes?"

"Harwell's tailor, as his label proclaims. All were finished and waiting in Kent, ready to be spirited into Harwell's own bedroom once police had found his body. But when you escaped, we brought everything to the Dover ferry and then onto this train."

"But if you expected Harwell on this train, there was no reason for you to bring garments that fit me."

"We were no longer expecting Harwell."

"Why not?"

"We learned that Lady Harwell had killed him. Your Mr. Holmes solved the case and had her arrested."

I shook my head, wondering how Holmes had become involved. "How did you learn that?"

"There are telephones at railway stations, Milord." She

smiled, and amusement shone in her dark eyes. "And I am still part of Sonnebourne's organisation. His funds have paid for this luxury that surrounds us. I suggest you take time to enjoy it. The waiter is hovering in the aisle behind you, eager to pour your champagne."

I watched as the waiter filled the crystal goblets, one for her, one for me. When he was out of earshot, I continued.

"If Harwell was dead, why send the clothes here?"

"Because we knew you were coming. Clegg heard you in the police station, warning someone about the Orient Express, just as he knocked the telephone from your hand. I saw you outside Victoria Station. And when you arrived in Dover, you asked about the ferry to Calais. And you certainly appeared to need help. You were unshaven and quite dishevelled."

"But why help me?"

"I told you. Because Mr. Holmes asked me to." She raised her glass. "Now, I propose a toast to your continued good health."

"Does Sonnebourne know I am here?"

"I reported to Sonnebourne from Victoria Station after I had seen you. I shall also send him a wire from Strasbourg."

My thoughts raced. "But he does not know you are working for Holmes?"

"If he did, I would be dead. Clegg would have killed me."

I kept my features steady. I had overheard Sonnebourne tell the other man, the dark-haired assassin, to do exactly that, but only after he had completed his deadly work of killing Holmes and the French Diplomat.

She paused and took out another cigarette from a flat silver case. "Holmes has caught wind of an assassination to be performed in Constantinople."

"By whom?"

"By me."

"I don't understand." I struck a match and lit her cigarette.

She reached across the table, touching my forearm lightly, with her fingertips. "I am the assassin, Dr. Watson. That is what I do for Sonnebourne."

I shuddered, but only inwardly. Keep her talking, I thought. "I find that hard to believe," I said.

"My most recent task involved a gullible woman, just before your abduction. She had no family and her appearance matched a client who wanted to be presumed dead. I drugged her, dressed her as a fortune-teller, led her to Westminster Bridge, and pushed her off. You may remember the case."

"I do. We thought Sonnebourne's organisation was behind it. Did Sonnebourne order you to kill your husband?"

"Kill Torrance, you mean?" She shook her head. "He was a repellent creature. Fortunately for me, he was never my husband. At the Grand Hotel, it was expedient for us to pass as a married couple. We did so for two very long years. When he was caught and jailed, I visited him. He wanted to kiss me goodbye, through the bars of his cell. Quite romantic. He closed his eyes as our lips met, and I broke his neck. As a doctor, you know exactly how that could be done."

Her matter-of-fact manner chilled me, though I tried not to show my revulsion. "I do. The cervical vertebrae are always vulnerable." I sipped champagne. "Now, what is your real name, if you are not Mrs. Torrance?"

"I have been called many names." She smiled, and her tone became softer, more sympathetic. "I have even been called a duchess. But I have no real name. I seem to outwear the ones I use from time to time. On this train, the name on my passport is Jane Griffin. Now you are wondering just what kind of monster fate has provided you as a travelling companion. Let me assure you, I am not a monster."

"So you will perform no more assassinations."

"I have promised Holmes."

"In Constantinople, who was the target?"

I knew the answer, of course: a French diplomat was the intended victim. But I would not reveal what I had overheard through the painting. That was my one advantage.

Her smile faded. "We will save that for our arrival. Now. I see the waiter's cart coming with our oysters and caviar. I must insist that we do not discuss business matters any further."

The cuisine of the Orient Express equalled the finest in my dining experience throughout my far-reaching adventures with Holmes. Yet I could not savour the rich fare. The woman now calling herself Jane Griffin sat before me, calmly enjoying her appetizers, her champagne, and then her soup, a lobster bisque that normally would have made me forget where I was. But I could not forget.

My thoughts were whirling. Was Jane Griffin really working for Holmes? Sonnebourne had said so, of course, in the conversation I had overheard. And why else would Jane Griffin claim that Holmes was now her ally? But still there was something troubling me. Something I could not put my finger on, but troubling nonetheless.

I had to learn more.

We were midway through the fourth course when I could restrain my concern no longer. "You promised to explain how you came to be working for Holmes."

She shook her finger in mock admonition. "That is going back to business."

"But for only a moment."

"Very well. For one moment only."

She set down her knife and fork, laying them neatly across the china plate with the Wagons-Lits emblem inlaid in gold. "Do you mean, how did Holmes find me? He would not disclose that."

I nodded. "Why didn't he have you arrested?"

"Because you had been abducted by then, and he wanted to rescue you. Under the circumstances, he said, he was prepared to bend the rule of law to serve a higher purpose."

"Not unheard of," I said.

"I told him I knew where you were."

"Did you mention Sonnebourne planned to use me as Harwell's corpse?"

"I did. Holmes was most anxious to prevent that."

"How?"

"He proposed a bargain. I was to help you escape. In Constantinople, I was to botch the assassination. And in return, he was to destroy Sonnebourne."

"Why would you want that?"

"Sonnebourne—" she broke off, turning away, her gaze directed at the window. Outside, the shadows of twilight lengthened and gathered, cloaking the green vista that sped endlessly towards us and then away.

After a few moments, she continued. "Sonnebourne is a slave master. I am his property. There is no leaving him. The police cannot defeat him. Holmes is my only hope."

18. WATSON

As the meal concluded nearly an hour later, the dessert, a rich crème brûlée, absorbed only a part of my attention. The surrounding conversation, the rhythmic click of the rails, the dusk that had turned to darkness outside—all faded into the background. The piano player had begun a familiar, sentimental tune, with lyrics that spoke of lost beauty and bygone love. I tapped my silver spoon to break through another layer of hardened caramelized sugar and then savoured the rich burnt-cream custard beneath. I thought of my dear wife, Mary. I wondered if I would have another chance at happiness with a lovely woman. It was the melancholy music, I told myself, that made me long for something different. I resolved simply to savour the moment, as Holmes had often advised.

Jane Griffin also had felt the nostalgia of the melody, I thought, for she put down her coffee cup and gave a sigh. "I will change my life," she said. "Though at my age, I wonder how much is possible."

Had I taken more champagne or brandy, I might have answered more sympathetically. I might have said that she was still a striking beauty. I might have said that her manners and movements would captivate whatever man became the object of her attention. But I said nothing. All I could think of was her cool description of how she had walked into a jail in the seaside town of Shellingford and killed her husband.

"Have you ever thought of starting again?" she asked.

"Sometimes," I had to admit.

"It is possible. If one has adequate means. Take our waiter, for example." She gestured at the man, smartly dressed as he was in his liveried uniform. "He is quite obviously a servant here. Possibly even ridiculous, you might think, in his silken hose and knee breeches and satin coat. Yet next month he will start anew. He will be his own master, opening his own hotel in Barcelona. The train abounds with opportunities, and he has been with the train for more than a decade. Nearly since it began."

"Able to save up a substantial sum, I suppose."

"Able to take advantage of opportunities," she replied.

"Are you suggesting that I do something different?"

"Oh, no. Certainly not now. You are loyal to Holmes. As am I. We are working together here, for a common purpose. I merely suggest that later, someday in the future, you might find yourself with an opportunity to strike out on your own."

"When the time comes, I will no doubt consider it," I said, sipping coffee.

She was looking at my right hand, which held the coffee cup. "Barked the skin on those knuckles, did you?"

"A little encounter with Clegg."

Her eyebrow lifted. "To judge from your unblemished features, you came out the winner. And Clegg is very good. You must be quite the fighter, Milord."

I had a realisation.

"Clegg will have telephoned Sonnebourne from Paris," I said.

She shrugged, as though the matter were of no consequence. "Undoubtedly."

"He will tell Sonnebourne that I am on the train, and that you facilitated my escape."

"And so?"

"Won't that put you in danger?"

She gave me a kindly smile. "I do appreciate your concern. But Sonnebourne was already aware of your presence. I told you, I reported to him from Dover. I spoke with him on the telephone."

"What did he say?"

"He intends for you to travel to Constantinople disguised as Lord Harwell. There is a room at the Pera Palace reserved for you. His plan is that you and Holmes—and by association, the British Government—will take the blame for the assassination."

I drew in my breath. "But you said—"

"That I was working for Holmes, and I am. There will be no assassination. Instead, I will take the payment money and vanish. Maybe you'll come with me."

The sentimental melody was concluding. I caught some of the words:

> But to me, you're as fair as you were, Maggie,
> When you and I were young.

"It's a thought," I said.

"You're a decent man," she said. "I wonder what would have happened."

"What?"

"If we'd met twenty years ago."

"I might have reformed you?"

"I might never have gone wrong." She smiled. "I was only eighteen."

"I was twenty-six," I said. "On a boat for India. On my way to Afghanistan. I was shot there."

"I am pleased that you came back."

* * *

We had stopped at Strasbourg when I said goodnight to the woman calling herself Jane Griffin and returned to my compartment. The attendant had already transformed my sofa into a bed. I ran my fingers over the silken sheets and held up the soft eiderdown pillow. But I had no time for sleep. I had to think. I needed to understand what might await me in Constantinople so I could warn Holmes.

I lifted my shade and peered outside my window, with the absurd notion that I might recognise someone. But only a uniformed railway attendant was on the platform. I realised that the train, being full, would not have passengers waiting to board, nor would a passenger on the Orient Express be likely to get off at the first stop from Paris. There were far less expensive ways to make that relatively short journey.

Beside the attendant was a tall table, resembling a speaker's podium. A second man approached, in a different uniform, carrying a valise. I saw his face. Maurice. I watched him walk up to the other attendant and place the valise on the podium. He opened the valise and took out a stack of leather folders resembling the passport Maurice had shown me earlier that evening. The attendant nodded, and Maurice returned the folders to the valise. Then I saw Jane Griffin on the platform, walking towards Maurice and the attendant. She handed the attendant a folded piece of yellow paper and a banknote. The two nodded. She returned to the train with Maurice. Her report to Sonnebourne, I thought.

A shrill whistle blew, and the train moved forward. As it picked up speed, I tried to focus my thoughts. What would happen in Constantinople?

The sleek-haired assassin was on his way. I might recognise him from behind, but I had not seen his face. I only knew Sonnebourne had ordered him to kill the diplomat, kill Holmes, and then kill the Torrance woman, who now called herself Jane Griffin.

But Jane Griffin had said she was the assassin. And, to help destroy Sonnebourne, she planned to steal the payment money and vanish. What would happen when she met the sleek-haired man? Would he kill her? Or would she kill him?

And what awaited me in Constantinople?

According to Jane Griffin, Holmes and I were to be blamed for the assassination. That was why Sonnebourne had paid for me to occupy this expensive compartment on this luxurious train. How would I be set up? Was someone waiting to attack me, as they had done in London? Or was there some other scheme?

What to do? What to believe? How to plan?

I seemed to hear Holmes's voice.

It is useless, even dangerous, to speculate until we have established the facts.

And there was one fact that I had to identify. One thread that might unravel the tangled web in which I found myself enmeshed.

I sat down on the bed, took out a pad and pen, wrote a telegraph message to Mycroft Holmes, and then coded it. In plain text the message read:

Mrs. Torrance now calling herself Jane Griffin. Says she is allied with Holmes. Please wire confirmation or denial, with instruction. Will arrive Wednesday at Pera Palace, Constantinople, under name of Harwell. JHW.

I rang for Maurice and handed him the message when he

arrived at my door a few moments later.

"Send from Munich, Milord?"

I nodded. "What time will that be?"

"Just past three in the morning, Milord."

"Then do not wake me."

I prepared for sleep. A few minutes later I was lying between silk sheets, clad in silk pyjamas, my head resting on a silk-covered eiderdown pillow. I closed my eyes, trying to empty my mind of the recent events that had somehow swept me away from London. I went over my telegram message. The code was a relatively easy one, involving a shift of letters in the alphabet. Mycroft had used it on a previous case, one in which I had been involved. Surely, he would recognise it and make short work of extracting my meaning.

But what if he did not?

No, that did not bear worrying about, I told myself. I had done all I could. The telegram would reach Mycroft, and Mycroft would reach Holmes, and Holmes would find a way to reach me when I arrived at the Pera Palace. Holmes would show me what to do.

The steel wheels beneath me clicked on the rails in a reassuring rhythm. The carriage swayed as though a rocking cradle. The cool night air fluttered the curtain at my window and made a refreshing change from the warm, tobacco-and-food-scented atmosphere of the dining car. I wondered where in Germany we were. I wondered if there were farms outside, or forests. I was tired, I told myself. I needed sleep. It ought to come immediately.

But it did not.

MONDAY, JULY 11

19. WATSON

I remained awake, more or less, tossing and turning. Then I realised that the click of the wheels had slowed, and the sway of the carriage had diminished. I heard the hiss of steam brakes. The train stopped. I sat up in the bed, noticing faint light coming through the small gap in the curtain. I stood and peered through the gap. Outside was a railway platform and a drab brick façade. A large painted sign proclaimed that this was 'München.' Munich. Shaded electric lamps illuminated the platform.

A uniformed attendant waited there. Once again, I saw Maurice approach, coming from the train. He passed the attendant a folded yellow paper—my message, I was sure of that. From a wallet Maurice extracted what appeared to be banknotes—likely those I had given him—and handed them over. The two men nodded, shook hands, and Maurice turned and walked back to the train, disappearing from my view. The transaction was complete, though I had not heard a single spoken word. The attendant remained on the platform, having pocketed the message and banknotes. I waited for him to go into the station, but he did not.

A moment later, another man appeared, also coming from the train, but from several cars forward of mine. His back to me, he handed the attendant a banknote. The attendant nodded and produced the yellow message paper Maurice had given him. The new arrival took the paper, opened it and glanced at the contents, holding it in one hand. The flame from a newly lit match flickered in his other hand. He touched the flame to the yellow paper. The two men watched it burn, first while held by the new arrival, and then on the concrete of the platform. The flame vanished. The attendant scuffed at the small remnants of embers and ash. The two men nodded at one another. The attendant stood by while the other turned back.

The other man's face was visible for only a moment. Then he was hurrying to the forward end of the train.

But in that moment, I recognised him.

Clegg.

The lights of the station faded away as the train gathered speed.

It took me several minutes to get dressed. At the end of the corridor, Maurice the carriage conductor was dozing on his chair. He looked up at me in surprise.

"Did you deliver my telegram?"

"Yes, Milord. At Munich. I handed it personally to the night manager. He was on the platform."

"Did you tell anyone you were delivering a message?"

"No, Milord."

I stepped around his chair. Tried the door. It was locked. "Maurice, I need to get through."

"The dining car is closed. The woman's lounge and the smoker are closed as well, Milord."

"I have some business with a passenger in third class."

For that was where Clegg would be, if he were on the train.

"Milord, they will be asleep."

I peeled off two hundred-franc notes and handed one to Maurice. "I shall be quite discreet," I said.

"You will pardon me, Milord, but you do not appear to be preparing for a quiet chat."

"I saw you give my message to the attendant in Munich. Then one of the third-class passengers bribed the attendant to hand it over. I watched him burn it and stamp out the ashes."

Maurice's eyes widened. "That is most irregular."

"So. May I pass, Monsieur Conductor?"

"Be careful, Milord. I cannot leave my post."

* * *

My after-dark transit from carriage to carriage was less disturbing than when I had first come on board, even though the wind howled around me and the rattle of the connecting chains and the wheels was just as loud. In the night, I was not distracted by the surrounding landscape whizzing by, or by the swift-moving ground beneath my feet. I had to press on. I had no choice but to confront Clegg. Holmes doubtless would have a better plan, but I needed to take action.

I passed through the dining room, where I pocketed a knife from one of the tables, and then the ladies' lounge and the men's smoker. Then I opened the door to the third-class carriage.

Lights were dimmed for sleeping, but I could see shadowy occupants slumped in their seats. There was also enough light for the seated conductor to recognise the hundred-franc note that I held before him.

I spoke in a low murmur. "I need a quiet word with one of the passengers. I will take him back to the smoking car so that we do not disturb the others."

The man nodded and tucked the banknote into his lapel pocket.

Clegg sat wide awake in the aisle seat across from where I stood. He was watching me.

"I heard," he said, getting to his feet. "Shall we go together, like gentlemen?"

The conductor opened the door for us and stood by in silence as we passed.

I palmed my knife as Clegg opened the smoking car door. We stood together for a moment as it clicked shut behind us.

"I think it's time we had a talk," I said.

He stepped back and moved to one of the upholstered chairs, next to a wall of books. He trailed his fingers casually along a shelf crowded with leather-bound spines. "Fine with me," he said, and sat. Then I saw the silver gun in his other hand.

"The conductor knows we're both in here," I said. "If one of us is found dead, the other will be the only suspect."

"And you're the one who's being hunted by the police. So you may as well put away that knife you're holding."

I sat in the chair across from him and placed the knife on the chair beside me. He did the same with his pistol.

"You burned my telegram," I said.

"I also got the two you tried to send from Paris. Where you mentioned the Pera Palace."

My heart sank. So Holmes and Mycroft would not know where I would be going. They would not know where to find me.

Unless.

If Holmes really was working with Jane Griffin, he would know where to find her. My spirit brightened, but I tried to mask my emotion. "How?"

"Telegraph clerks don't get paid very well."

"So you were watching for me in Paris."

"Also in London. Who do you think hit you from behind, and planted you for the Lavender Hill police to discover? I interrupted your telephone call too, but you already knew that. It was my job. But it was also my job to let you get away."

"You let me escape?"

"Did you think you were so accomplished a fighter, Dr. Watson?" He smiled. "At Cambridge, I played on the rugby and fencing and boxing teams. I have kept in trim since."

I shook my head. "I thought you were a street thug."

His voice now had a mocking tone, with an exaggerated Cockney accent. "Because me 'ead was shaved? Because I said I would get a bit o' me own back?" Then he shrugged and spoke once again in the voice of an educated man. "I thought you might have spotted my manicured fingernails. But no matter. It's only business, after all. Nothing personal."

"You're only doing your job."

"Sonnebourne gives me the orders."

"What orders, exactly?"

"I am to prevent you from sending telegrams, but to allow you to proceed to Constantinople."

"What if I try to escape?"

"You won't get far. I have copies of the British newspapers to show the authorities. With your pretty picture."

"What happens to me in Constantinople?"

"I do not become involved. I return when I have handed you off to the woman."

"Mrs. Torrance."

"Mrs. who?" Clegg's blank look appeared genuine.

"The woman in Paris. The woman who ordered you to let me board this train."

"Ah. Hadn't heard that one. She has many names."

"The Duchess?"

He said nothing.

"What about Griffin?"

He shrugged.

"What happens to Holmes?"

He did not seem at all surprised by my question. "I won't be around to see it, but I do know. The woman will kill him when she kills the other."

"The Frenchman."

"The political target."

"Why Holmes?"

"He stole a valuable painting from Lord Sonnebourne, and that theft cannot go unpunished."

"Why do you work for a man like Sonnebourne?"

"Someday I won't," he said.

"You mean someday you'll have a lot of money?"

"Oh, I have money now. I'll quit Sonnebourne when I'm good and ready. Time hasn't come yet."

"You're waiting for something."

He smiled. "Tell you what. If you survive, you can look me up. Roland Clegg. They called me 'Childe Roland' at school. My face, you see. Not quite as pretty as some. Ironic. Anyway, I have no other name. The Cambridge registrar will have an address for me."

"If I survive."

"Now I suggest we return, like gentlemen, to our respective carriages. You are guaranteed safe passage to Constantinople."

I picked up my knife. He picked up his gun. Warily, we backed away from one another.

He shook a warning finger, only partly in jest. "No more telegrams."

"Until Constantinople," I said. Then I asked, "Did Maurice tell you?"

"That you would send a telegram? No. The woman told me."

20. LUCY

I paused now and again as I made my way through the London Streets, listening for sounds of footsteps from behind. The back of my neck crawled with the urge to turn and look, but I forced myself to keep my eyes focused straight ahead.

My night's worth of evasions and costume changes had taken several hours. Dawn was beginning to tinge the edges of the sky and the tops of the brick buildings with red as I came up Warwick Street. The pavements were growing more crowded as night laborers and peddlers straggled home from their work, while the rest of the city woke up to a new day.

Eccleston Square, though, was only about a block ahead of me and was still deserted at this early hour of the morning. A private garden associated with the Pimlico housing development, the square was enclosed by a thick shrubbery. Tall trees lined the pathways that crisscrossed the garden's central lawn, casting dark shadows.

I veered across Saint George Street and entered the park.

Immediately, stillness and the eerie feeling of isolation closed in, despite the busy London streets surrounding the garden on all sides. The leaves above me rustled in the early-morning breeze. My footsteps echoed and the cold prickles at the back of my neck intensified, but I kept walking—until a man's voice came from behind me.

"Stop right there."

I turned around slowly.

The man who confronted me was of medium height and build, dressed in a nondescript brown suit and bowler hat. His face was hard to make out, shadowed by the trees overhead. But his features looked to be remarkably average, as well: somewhere between thirty and forty with rounded cheeks and an unshaven chin. In short, he was the ideal candidate for surveillance, someone who would blend easily into a crowd and pass unnoticed.

He was also pointing a Colt .45 revolver at my chest.

"Don't move."

My heart rate picked up, but I felt a wash of relief, as well. I had been afraid that this night's excursion really would be an exercise in futility and wasted shoe-leather.

"Who are you?" I asked. "Want to do you want?" I didn't add that if only he had approached me earlier, it would have saved a great deal of trouble and time.

"You're to come with me." Despite his size, the man had a surprisingly deep voice, tinged with gravel.

"I don't think so. But I will make you a counter-proposal: why don't you tell me exactly who hired you for this job and what you know about them?"

The man was fighting to maintain the stolidity of his expression, but I saw the flicker of surprise register in his gaze. Plainly he had imagined this confrontation going differently.

"I'm the one with the gun." He still wasn't near enough for him to try and grab me; I'd been keeping a close eye on the distance between us. But he made a threatening wave with the revolver. "That means you do what I tell you to."

"Again, I don't think so."

The entire purpose of tonight's expedition had been to draw out our enemies and allow me to come face to face with someone who would—we hoped—be in a position of power high enough that they would know the answers to the questions that plagued this entire venture.

That was why I had allowed the old man back in Baker Street to come close enough that he would hear my directions to the cabbie—directions that I'd purposely given in a clear voice, before entering the cab. It was why I'd lingered a short while in the church and in the coffee house and in Holmes' bolt hole: to allow anyone following me to contact their superiors.

I'd walked and ridden around half of London tonight, putting on a convincing show of someone trying to lose a pursuer—all the while leaving a small trail of breadcrumbs behind that those keeping watch on me could follow.

The question was whether I'd succeeded, and whether or not the man pointing the gun at me now was a mere minor cog in the wheel, or someone higher up in Lord Sonnebourne's organisation. Studying his bland, anonymous features, I couldn't be sure.

His clothes were of cheap quality, but they could have been purchased especially for his current purpose. His voice was rough and uneducated—but as I knew better than anyone, voices and accents could be easily assumed and discarded again. The guarded intelligence that lay at the back of his light-coloured eyes gave me hope that this exercise hadn't been completely in vain.

"I could just shoot you right here," he growled. He spoke with a shade less certainty than before, although the gleam of enjoyment in his eyes told me that he was no stranger to violence.

Unless I was much mistaken, he had taken lives before tonight and enjoyed it.

Breeze stirred the trees again, and an owl's low call came from the dense trees somewhere close by.

I decided to try a gamble. "We both know that if you had permission to shoot me, you would have done it by now. You obviously have instructions to capture me and bring me to whoever is giving you your orders. I want to know who that someone is, to begin with. And you can go on by telling me who among your people is travelling to Constantinople by way of the Orient Express."

I'd been right; this time, he couldn't suppress the shock that etched his features into a momentarily blank mask. Then his expression hardened.

"And you think you can somehow make me tell you that?" He gave me a dismissive look, upper lip curled. "You, on your own?"

He might have been surprised. All the while we'd been talking, I had been making silent calculations. His average height and muscle mass were in my favour. He still outweighed me, but I estimated that I had about a seventy-five percent chance of success if I stepped forward under his guard, knocked his gun hand up, kicked his leg out from under him, and then delivered a hard chop to his throat on the way down.

But I would only go that route as a last resort.

"Maybe not." I spoke pleasantly. "But I think the odds are fairly good that he can."

As I spoke, Jack stepped out of the bushes just behind the stranger, seized him, and with a quick jerk of motion yanked the revolver from his hand.

He'd moved so fast that the man was still gaping in astonishment when he found himself with one arm twisted up behind him and Jack's forearm clamped across his throat.

"Thank you." I smiled at Jack before addressing the man in the brown suit again. "You know, it's remarkable how frequently those who are intent on following a mark will completely neglect to take into account the fact that someone else could be following them."

Jack had left Becky in the care of Mrs. Hudson, and had been following after me since Baker Street. A police sergeant's uniform was nearly as good as a false beard and glasses for remaining anonymous. Those intending to break the law had only to see Jack's blue tunic and brass buttons before deciding to stay as far away from him as possible.

The owl's call had been our signal that he was here and in position.

Jack tightened his arm across the stranger's throat. "I think the lady asked you a question. You can answer it now. Or I can arrest you for attempted abduction, and you can answer that and a lot of other questions at Scotland Yard. Your choice."

The man's face twisted, anger replacing shock as he struggled in Jack's grip. But the anger ebbed quickly when he found that Jack's hold on him didn't slacken, and when he spoke the words were thready with fear.

"You don't understand! She will kill me if I talk to the rozzers!"

Now that he was captive, his voice had changed slightly, the accent of East London becoming tinged with something else, something that sounded Eastern European. Born in one of the Balkan states and emigrated to London as a child would be my guess.

"We can keep you safe," I told him. "But who is she?" We were aware already that the woman we knew as Mrs. Torrence was high up in Sonnebourne's organisation, but we didn't have either her real identity or her current whereabouts.

The stranger's eyes were so wide I could see the whites gleaming in the dawn light.

"You think you are a match for her?"

From the nearby Victoria Station, a train's shrill whistle cut the park's stillness. The man's head lifted, then his face twisted again. "She'll kill you, too!"

Jack's grasp still had him immobilized, but he managed to raise one hand, bringing it to his mouth in a movement so lightning quick it took me a split second to even register.

"Jack!"

My warning came too late. The man had already bitten down on something, and now his face changed, contorting horribly as he choked and gasped. His whole body went rigid, then collapsed.

Swearing under his breath, Jack lowered him to the ground and worked over him, tilting his head back and trying to clear his airway.

I shook my head. "It's too late." The stranger's face was blue-tinged and his breath had already stopped. "He's dead. He must have taken cyanide."

"My fault," Jack said. Grim frustration tightened his mouth. "I checked to make sure he didn't have any other weapons, but I never thought about poison."

"It's not your fault. Cyanide never occurred to me, either." I tensed against a shiver as I crouched down next to Jack and examined the dead man. "He must have had it hidden in his ring."

I gestured to the heavy signet ring the man wore on his left hand. The stone was flipped up to reveal a Lucrezia Borgia-style compartment for poison.

"It's like something out of bad quality sensational fiction—except that it's real."

We had also just run solidly into the proverbial dead end. The sky was lightening, and the train to Dover would be leaving from Victoria Station soon.

Jack nodded, even though I hadn't spoken out loud. "You need to go or you'll miss your train. I'll take care of this and see it gets reported to the Yard."

He stood up, gesturing to the body at our feet.

I still felt chilled, even though the early morning air wasn't especially cool. "Thank you." I managed a smile as I straightened up, too. "It appears there are some advantages to being married to a policeman."

"Just a few?"

I leaned against him for a moment. "Possibly several."

Jack put his arm around me. "You've got everything you need?"

"I have the false identity papers from Mycroft." They were sewn into the lining of my jacket. "And Flynn has already checked a trunk for me at the Victoria Station baggage claim. All I have to do is give them the claims ticket."

I couldn't maintain a male disguise in the close quarters of a train, where people would see me up close, so the young man would vanish on the way to Dover in the private train carriage that was also already booked for me, to be replaced by Clarice Earnshaw, the name on my identity papers.

Jack and I had been over the details before, but I could tell he didn't want to let me go any more than I wanted to leave.

Finally, though, Jack bent down and rested his forehead against mine. "Come back to me, all right?"

I nodded, shutting my eyes. "I promise I'll do my absolute best."

21. WATSON

I returned to my compartment and slept fitfully. Amid the clatter of the wheels and swaying of the car, I caught the scent of tobacco smoke.

I came awake to find Sherlock Holmes seated at the foot of my bed.

Cross-legged in his contemplative or meditative posture, clad in his smoking jacket, he sat upon a stack of embroidered pillows, a magnifying lens in one hand and a long cigarette holder in the other. His hair appeared blacker and sleeker than when I had last seen him. I wondered if he had put on one of his theatrical disguises in order to gain admission to the train. "You find yourself boxed in, old friend," he said. "You are wondering what to do."

Then I noticed that he and his pillows floated nearly a foot above my silk bedclothes.

"Holmes," I said, "you are not real. You are a figment of my distressed imagination. You are no more than a residue of the over-rich crème brûlée I consumed some hours ago."

"That is a medical explanation," he replied. "A more advanced theory would be that your own imagination has brought up the image that you wish for, in response to your frustrated attempt to reach me by telegram. Pray, question me, then, old friend, as you wish. I am at your service."

"This is folly," I said.

"Not at all. You know my methods. You have often remarked that I make deductions from signs that are so subtle and minute that they go unnoticed. I am here to tell you that you have seen such signs—and heard them, I might add—but you have not observed with sufficient acuity as to extract the full measure of their value."

"Even in my dreams, Holmes, you are most annoying."

"Hardly my fault, then, you must admit, if you yourself are creating the annoyance. But let us state the problem. You wish to question me, because you need to know if the woman who now calls herself Jane Griffin remains an enemy, or if she has become my ally. You are restrained by Clegg, who has orders to prevent you from questioning me by telegram. And Sonnebourne's people have framed you for two murders, so you cannot get help from the authorities."

"That is all true, Holmes. But what am I to do about it?" My voice rose and I sat up in my bed.

Holmes and his pillows floated undisturbed above the covers.

I went on, "Are you working with Jane Griffin or are you not? I must know if I can trust her! She may kill you! So, do not be coy with me!"

Holmes took a delicate puff on the cigarette and exhaled a series of perfect smoke rings, each concentrically expanding around the next. "The Torrance woman is your answer," he said.

"You mean I should ask her whether she is telling me the truth? But her trustworthiness is the very essence of the problem! Holmes, that is too much, even from you."

His eyes widened, and he gave a sympathetic nod. "Nevertheless, old friend, I say that the Torrance woman is your answer."

From my compartment door came a soft tapping.

And a voice. Maurice's voice. "Milord?"

Holmes's floating form grew cloudy, and then transparent.

"Holmes!" I cried. "Holmes!"

"Farewell, old friend," he said, and vanished. My compartment was dark.

The tapping noise became a knock. "Milord? Are you there?"

22. WATSON

At breakfast I confronted Jane Griffin.

We were near Vienna. Bright sunlight streamed in through the tall windows, and the dining car seemed larger and airier than before, with its high-arched and artfully decorated ceiling now clearly visible. On the sparkling white linen tablecloth was local fare: bread rolls with butter and marmalade, muesli, bacon, and boiled egg. Normally I would have had a good appetite. Now, I took only black coffee, which was powerful and steaming hot. We were at one of the tables for two, alongside the window. I kept my voice low so that the couple across the aisle would not overhear our conversation over the rumble and muted clatter of the carriage on the rails.

"Clegg is on the train," I said.

"Third class."

"You told Clegg of my telegram."

"Of course I told Clegg. He reports to Sonnebourne."

"Clegg destroyed my message."

She shrugged and took a delicate sip of coffee leaving a faint trace of lip rouge around the gold-edged rim of the fine-china cup. "Those were his instructions."

"Aren't you curious as to what I said?"

"It does not matter."

"I was reporting to Holmes."

"Only fair, since I must report to Sonnebourne."

"By telegram?"

She lifted the small crystal vase from our table and toyed with the single pink rose. "I left the train. I can do that, since police are not looking for me."

"Have you tried sending a message to Holmes?"

"Not possible, with him enroute to Constantinople. But I shall try tomorrow from Belgrade. He may be at the Pera Palace by then. He is to meet us there when we arrive Wednesday morning." She smiled. "I am sure he will be pleased to see you."

* * *

I had lunch in my compartment. My sleepless night, my pre-dawn encounter with Clegg, and my exasperating dream of Holmes had left me in need of rest. I was determined to carry on. I obtained a guidebook to Constantinople from Maurice. I studied it. It was in French, and so I learned little. I tried to memorize the map, which showed the locations of the railway station and the Pera Palace Hotel. They looked about a half-hour's walk from one another. Then I dozed, half-wondering if I would dream of Holmes again. But I did not. I woke as we pulled into Budapest station. As I dressed for dinner, I thought of Jane Griffin. I would not have many more opportunities to question her. In a day and a half, we would be in Constantinople and at least one assassin would be preparing to kill Holmes and the French diplomat. Would she also be a victim of the sleek-haired man I had seen across the desk from Sonnebourne?

23. LUCY

The train's whistle blew a sharp blast. The wheels began to move, and the Gare de l'Est platform receded as the train pulled out of the station.

I was in Paris—or had been, until the train's departure a moment ago, having caught the early morning train at Victoria that had brought me to Dover, and from there taken the ferry across the channel to Calais.

Now I was at last on the Compagnie Internationale des Wagons-Lits train commonly known as the Orient Express. I leaned back against the cushioned seat in my sleeping compartment and shut my eyes. Thanks to Mycroft, I once again had my own private compartment, and like everything else about the train, the small chamber was of luxurious quality. The walls were of dark panelled wood. The seat that could be folded out into a bed at night was covered with velvet and eminently comfortable. But however tired I was, my nerves were too on-edge for me to rest.

I had seen only a few of my fellow passengers so far and only in passing, but I was fairly certain that none of them had been Holmes, even in disguise. For safety's sake, Mycroft hadn't told me the name and persona under which Holmes would be travelling—and apart from ruling out the two baggage cars, he could now be in any of the berths on the train.

Assuming that he had made it onto the train. He could have

been attacked in London, or at any point in his own journey from London to Dover and on to Calais.

I snapped that line of thinking off. Unlike my own evasive measures, Holmes' movements before leaving London would have been genuinely designed to throw off pursuit. And there was no one better at shaking a follower off than Sherlock Holmes.

I stood up, splashed water from the pitcher into the wash basin, washed my face and combed my hair. Then I changed out of my travelling clothes and into the ruffled pink silk dress that I—or rather Clarice Earnshaw—had chosen for evening wear.

The restaurant carriage was at the far end of my train carriage. I made my way there along the narrow aisle that ran alongside the individual sleeping compartments, nearly bumping into a tall, grey-haired man in the robes of a Roman Catholic priest. He gave me a disapproving look from under bushy grey brows that suggested he found my dress and jewellery to be sinfully expensive at best, immodest at worst. Then he muttered something unintelligible and disappeared into the sleeping compartment two doors down from mine.

Despite it being the dinner hour, the restaurant car when I reached it wasn't crowded, with only about half of the white-clothed tables occupied. The train must not be fully booked with passengers.

I took a seat at an empty table near to the door and surveyed the room.

Two stout men of middle-aged and prosperous appearance were seated at a table near the end of the car and were deep in a discussion in Italian that included raised voices and a multitude of hand-gestures.

A slim younger man was seated a few tables away from them.

His clothes were of the best Saville Row quality, and he had fair hair, a weak chin, and peered at the world through a monocle. Only if he had *British Aristocracy* tattooed in ink across his forehead could his background have been more clear.

Although those details were easy enough to fake. I was currently dressed to look like the young man's female equivalent—an English society miss, brought up to believe that life was one long round of balls and tea parties and London society seasons.

To that end, my wedding ring was gone, left behind in London in case of anyone's searching my luggage. Wigs and other elements of false disguise were as difficult to maintain long-term and in close quarters as male apparel would have been. But I had coloured both my eyebrows and my hair with henna. It would eventually wash out, but for now my usually dark brown hair had reddish mahogany highlights, and I had arranged it in a riot of curls that had caused me to burn myself three times with the curling tongs.

I continued my study of the dining car's occupants. At the table next to mine sat a middle-aged woman with iron grey hair and a weather-beaten, formidable face: determined jaw, broad nose and cheekbones, and piercing dark eyes. She was currently taking a waiter to task for the fact that she had been brought coffee with sugar, when in fact she had requested it black.

"Yes, Lady Danville. Right away, Lady Danville. That is, I shall bring you another cup straight away." The waiter bowed hasty apologies and made his escape, bearing away the offending coffee cup.

The only other occupants of the restaurant car sat at the two tables across the aisle from mine. They appeared to be a family party: a father with sleek dark hair and a walrus moustache, and his daughter, who shared her father's colouring and looked to be seven or eight. I doubted that the lady sitting with the child was the mother, though. She was somewhere in her middle thirties, and her plain brown dress and severe, entirely unornamented hairstyle clearly proclaimed governess.

At the moment, she was endeavouring to get her charge to eat her dinner—a vain effort, because the little girl was sitting with her arms folded and her face set in a ferocious scowl, kicking her heels against the bottom of her chair.

"Come, Rosamund, just try one bite?" the governess cajoled in a sing-song voice. "Just one tiny little bite? It's lovely rice pudding, see? And you'll never grow big and strong if you don't eat, you know."

The governess no doubt meant well, but in the child Rosamund's place, I would have refused to do anything asked of me in that tone of voice just on principle.

"I said I don't want it!"

Rosamund had almost Spanish colouring: lightly tanned skin, dark hair and long-lashed dark eyes set under very straight dark brows. Her face was square jawed, and was probably determined-looking even when she was in the best of tempers—which at the moment she patently was not.

"I won't eat it, I won't!" She shoved the dish of rice pudding across the table, nearly catapulting it onto her governess's lap. "Father—I don't like the food on this train! Tell Miss Nordstrom that she can't make me eat it! Tell her!"

Her father held a newspaper spread open in front of him and appeared to be paying no attention whatever to either his daughter or Miss Nordstrom. But at Rosamund's address he lowered the paper just enough to give his daughter a quick glance.

"Do as Miss Nordstrom says, Rosamund."

His voice was curt, and the moment he'd spoken, he once more raised the newspaper, forming an effective barrier between himself and his two companions.

Rosamund looked at him a moment, then scowled harder, kicking her feet with extra emphasis.

"There, you see?" Anyone who had the smallest degree of experience with children ought to have known that silence in that moment was by far the best policy. Miss Nordstrom was either new to her job or extremely bad at it, because she pounced on her employer's words with beaming triumph and went on in the same chirping tone. "Now, come along, just a teensy little bite?"

Instead of answering, Rosamund jumped up—this time knocking over the glass that had contained her milk—and bolted from the restaurant car.

Miss Nordstrom's brow puckered in distress. She dabbed helplessly and ineffectually at the puddle of spilled milk with a napkin, then murmured something about going after the child before hurrying from the carriage.

Rosamund's father didn't reply or even glance up from his newspaper.

"That child is abominably spoiled."

I looked up to find that the grey-haired woman Lady Danville was addressing me from the table next to mine.

"Do you think so?" I glanced at Rosamund's father again. Our voices were covered by the continual clatter of the train's wheels and the chug of the engine, but in any case, Rosamund's father appeared as oblivious to our conversation as he had been to his daughter's departure. He spared us not a single glance.

"I am certain of it!" Lady Danville said.

Now that I had a chance to study her more closely, I remembered that I had seen her before. Not in person, but her name appeared in the papers in association with various charitable works. Her husband, Lord Danville, was a member of Parliament, and with his backing, Lady Danville championed projects to create more schools and better housing amongst the poorest neighbourhoods of London's East End.

A formidable woman—but then she would have to be in order to accomplish any tangible results in Whitechapel or Limehouse. And certainly no one could claim that reforms in those areas were not desperately needed.

She, too, glanced across the restaurant car's aisle, then lowered her voice. "We were staying at the same hotel in Paris for the past two days before the train's departure, and I had the chance to make a study of the family. That governess creature simply hasn't any backbone at all. The child misbehaves, and she does nothing whatsoever about it. I always insisted on hiring German governesses for my own children when they were small. Whatever else one may say of the Germanic people, they do understand proper order and discipline! But that child Rosamund is constantly allowed to get her own way in everything."

From what little I had seen of them, I would have said that the answer to Rosamund's troubles was more complicated than a simple case of being spoiled. But I didn't voice the opinion out loud.

"Who is her father, do you know?"

Lady Danville got up from her seat and came to join me at my table. "May I?"

I acquiesced with a nod, and Lady Danville went on, nodding

to Rosamund's father.

"His last name is Anstruther. He is a widower, and I believe he is something to do with the diplomatic service—going out to protect our interests in this trouble they seem to be having over the Suez Canal."

The mention of the Suez made my nerves prickle, even though a less likely conspirator than Lady Danville could scarcely have been imagined.

"He travels all over the world, and so the child is dragged here, there, and everywhere. And her father can't be bothered to see that she has any kind of proper training." Lady Danville sniffed disapproval.

Mr. Anstruther must care about his daughter, though, otherwise he would have left her in a boarding school while he went abroad, instead of bringing her with him. I'd grown up in an establishment like that, with several of my classmates being the daughters of highly-placed diplomats.

"And you?" I asked. "Are you travelling all the way to Constantinople?"

"Yes. I am joining my daughter, whose husband works for the foreign office and is stationed in the embassy there. She is expecting her second child, and I am going out to lend a hand with things after the birth."

At the mentioned of her daughter and grandchild, Lady Danville unbent perceptibly, even going so far as to show me a sepia photograph of her daughter and her daughter's little boy—a curly haired child of two or three.

"And you, my dear?" she asked, when she had stowed the photograph away once more. "I hope that you're not travelling all the way to Constantinople alone?"

As a young, unmarried female, travelling such a distance on my own would indeed be something of a scandal.

"I'm afraid so. Originally, my aunt was to accompany me, but she took ill at the last moment and couldn't come after all. I'm travelling out to join my father. His regiment is stationed in Syria, but he's coming to meet me in Constantinople. He only has leave to come and meet me for a short while—that was why it was important that I not miss the train or delay the journey for another time."

"Your father is with the army?"

"Yes, General Earnshaw."

Mycroft's connections had elicited the information that there was indeed a General Earnshaw currently serving in the army at one of Britain's more obscure outposts in Syria. But there hadn't been time to create a deeper or more complete cover story for me than that.

Now I had to hope that I wouldn't have the spectacularly bad luck to discover that Lady Danville was in fact acquainted with that gentleman.

She merely nodded, though. "Well, my dear, you must allow me to look after you, especially if this is your first journey abroad. The way these foreigners will try to take advantage of one is simply shocking—especially a young girl, travelling alone."

Gaining Lady Danville as a chaperone could prove inconvenient if she wanted to keep an eye on my every movement. But it might also have its advantages.

"Do you know any of the other passengers on the train?" I asked.

As I had suspected, Lady Danville did indeed. She was of the type who, though not at all malicious or a gossip, simply considers everyone else's business to be her own. And she was only too happy to share her knowledge. "Well, as I told you, the child Rosamund's father is something to do with the diplomatic service. Then there is a Roman Catholic Priest."

"I saw him earlier," I volunteered. "He has the compartment two doors down from mine."

Lady Danville inclined her head in acknowledgment. "He told me when we were boarding the train that he runs a mission in Constantinople and was returning after having been in England to raise funds. Ordinarily, I do not approve of Catholics; however, he seemed perfectly sincere."

"What about that gentleman over there?" I nodded to the fair-haired Englishman with the monocle—who so far was leaving his dinner untouched, but was making rapid progress through the bottle of wine that the waiter had brought to accompany his food.

"That is the Honourable Richard Mallowe." Lady Danville's brows pinched with disapproval. "You would be well advised to stay away from him, my dear. Despite his title, he is not a respectable person to know."

That was truer than Lady Danville probably knew. I hadn't recognised the Honourable Mr. Mallowe by sight, but the society pages were frequently plastered with his exploits, which ranged from public drunkenness—he had once while heavily inebriated attempted to swim in the Trafalgar Square fountain—to scandalous liaisons with other men's wives.

However—and the fact made me study Mr. Mallowe with more interest—he had of late come within the range of Holmes's attention, owing to some of his most recent affairs skating across the line into illegality. His name had come up in association with an illegal gambling den in the Seven Dials district, and also with a scheme of fixing horse races. He was, so rumour had it, heavily in debt, with his family's estate mortgaged and his creditors closing in.

In short, he was an ideal candidate for one of Lord Sonnebourne's promises of a new identity and a new life away from the crimes of the old one.

Lady Danville was still speaking. "Those two gentlemen are Italians, and don't speak a word of English as far as I can tell. I don't know what their business abroad is."

I could have told her that from what I could gather they were in the business of importing wine, and were lamenting the drought that had caused a sharp decrease in the quality of this year's grape harvest. But Clarice Earnshaw wasn't supposed to be able to speak or understand Italian.

"And those are all of the passengers in the first-class carriage," Lady Danville included. "Apart from an Austrian viscount. Count Styptovich, I believe the name was. A very elderly gentleman, and quite infirm. I saw three of the Wagons-Lits attendants helping him to board the train, and one of them told me that he had requested all of his meals to be served to him in his compartment, as his health was too fragile for him to make the journey to the dining car."

Our waiter brought me a menu at that point, and the rest of the meal passed with me answering Lady Danville's questions about my own upbringing and background. It was difficult to give my full attention to making sure that I kept my details straight and didn't contradict myself. Our conversation had given me a great deal to think about.

24. WATSON

At seven that evening the train had just left Budapest. I went to the dining car refreshed, prepared with a line of questioning.

Jane Griffin sat at the table we had previously occupied, wearing a crème-coloured silk dress. A small crème-coloured matching hat was pinned to her tightly coiffed black hair.

I began my questions with, "Do you always work alone on Sonnebourne's projects?"

"Why do you ask?"

"I wondered if there were others."

"No others."

"Sonnebourne may have sent reinforcements."

She shrugged. "We should talk of something more pleasant."

"If I am to be helpful, I should know what to expect."

"I shall tell you when we meet Holmes on Wednesday. Less than two days from now."

I was not about to be put off. "So you always work alone?"

"Once or twice I have been part of a team."

"Which team member would Sonnebourne send?"

"I have no idea."

"None at all? What would you do if you were Sonnebourne?"

She smiled. "What a persistent fellow you are, Milord." Then her tone softened. "I suppose, if I were Sonnebourne, I would send someone I thought would blend in with the surrounding populace. A Turk."

"A man? Or a woman?"

"For the railway station, a man. Able to shoulder his way through the crowds and make his escape."

"Any man in particular?"

She lifted the evening's table flower—another rose—and brandished it playfully in my face before tucking it away into its crystal goblet. "I am thinking you wish to trick me in some way, Milord."

I spread my palms. "Generally, women think I am not at all devious. Quite the opposite, in fact."

"Very well, I shall trust you." She poured ice water for us both into heavy crystal glasses. "The man I worked with— I saved his life in Sofia, nearly five years ago. He is tall, thin, elegantly handsome, clean shaven and well-groomed. His hair is jet black."

"Not unlike Mr. Holmes."

"He is called Malat, because he comes from the town of Malatya."

So the sleek-haired man I had seen with Sonnebourne had a name. And she had saved his life. And now he would be coming to kill her.

"But there will be dozens more resembling him at the station," she went on. "Come, do not look so downcast. When we arrive, I will show you the station and where the target will be. You can understand what is to transpire. By the way, Clegg will be there as well."

I sipped ice water. "I thought Clegg planned to return immediately. On this very train."

"He told you that?" She smiled.

"Why will he be at the station?"

"Sonnebourne's orders are to make sure you attend a certain political event that will occur there Friday afternoon. Then Clegg and I are to kill you."

I raised my palms in mock horror. "But you have promised Holmes that there will be no assassination."

Her smile broadened. "Would it count as an assassination if I were to kill Clegg?"

25. LUCY

I was back in my own compartment, sitting on the edge of the bed that the conductor had just made up for me, when the door opened.

I stiffened, my hand moving instinctively towards the pistol that I had already placed under the pillow. But the figure that slipped through my open door was small, dressed in a lacy white nightgown—and wearing a prodigious scowl.

Rosamund drew up short at the sight of me, her eyes rounding in surprise. "Oh. I thought this compartment was empty."

"I think you want the next one down," I told her. I had already discovered that the Austrian Archduke's compartment was next to mine, on the side nearest to the front of the train. But the one on the other side of me, closer to the back of the train, was unoccupied. "Why do you need an empty compartment?"

Rosamund gave me an appraising look as though trying to decide whether or not to trust me, then stuck out her lower lip. "To hide from Miss Nordstrom. She's trying to put me to bed."

"And I suppose you're not tired yet?" Experience with Becky had taught me that children could be asleep on their feet and yet vociferously deny feeling the slightest bit of fatigue.

"Not at all! So I told her that I had to go to the washroom." A small hint of satisfaction crept into Rosamund's tone. "Then I came in here before she could come out of our compartment and see where I'd gone."

"I see. She'll probably be worried about you, when you don't come back and she can't find you, though."

Rosamund shrugged, scuffing her bare toes against the carpet.

I studied her for a second, then reached for the tin that the Wagons-Lits attendant had placed on the shelf by the bed. "There are some biscuits here. Would you like one? I think I saw some chocolate ones."

Rosamund's eyes flashed to mine again, her look wary, eyes narrowed in suspicion. "You're not going to march me straight back to Miss Nordstrom?"

"Not right away, at least." I opened the tin and offered it to her. "You can sit down, too, if you'd like."

After a moment's hesitation, Rosamund accepted both a biscuit and the invitation, perching on the end of the bed and curling her feet up under her.

"You're nicer than those Italian men. I accidentally opened the door to their compartment after dinner, and one of them shouted at me to get out. As if I'd want to stay in their nasty compartment anyway!" She made a face. "It smelled like my father does when he's had too much to drink—mixed with old socks!"

I smiled, waiting as Rosamund licked a smear of chocolate from her fingers, then said, "You know, the odd thing is, I'm certain that I locked the door to my compartment before you came in."

Rosamund startled, the wary, sullen look once more coming down over her small features. "Maybe you forgot to."

"I'm quite sure that I didn't." I spoke gently, though, and after a moment, Rosamund gave up, letting out a defeated sigh.

"Fine. I stole this from one of the attendants when he came

in to make up our beds for the night." She held up a pass key, of the kind that the Wagons-Lits conductors wore on their belts to open any door on the train. Her small face settled in a sulky frown. "I suppose now you're going to say that I have to give it back."

"No." If nothing else, I had to admire what seemed to be an inborn skill at picking pockets. I had had to practice for months before I could lift a man's watch or key chain without his noticing.

"You're not?" Rosamund was so shocked that she forgot momentarily to look sullen.

"Not for the moment. You have to promise me that you won't go into any more compartments that belong to other people, though. It's not good manners."

It could also be dangerous. I didn't know whether Holmes and I were being observed on the train. Everyone on board with us might be exactly who they claimed to be. But if one of the passengers wasn't what he or she seemed—and if Rosamund stumbled on that potentially deadly secret—

"I'll make you a list of the empty compartments," I told her. "But you also have to promise not to be gone so long that Miss Nordstrom gets into a panic about you."

Rosamund's expression was a blend of relief warring with suspicion. "Why are you being so nice to me?"

"Because everyone needs to get away by themselves now and again. And because I like you."

"No you don't." Rosamund's chin dropped to her chest, and she wrapped her arms around herself. "No one likes me."

She spoke with flat, matter-of-fact certainty that was far sadder than tears or a plea for sympathy would have been.

Telling her that it couldn't be true or that I was certain she was wrong would do no good at all. I settled for a question. "No one?"

Rosamund crumbled a piece of biscuit between two fingers, looking down at the carpet. "Well, Miss Nordstrom doesn't like me. She looks after me because father pays her to, but she thinks I'm horrible."

"How long has Miss Nordstrom been looking after you?" I asked.

"Since my mother died. Last year." Rosamund's voice was once again flatly unemotional—but not, I was sure, because she actually felt nothing.

"What about your father?" I asked. I had the sense of treading on dangerous ground, so I kept my tone mild, my words careful. "He'll probably be wondering where you've gotten to by now."

"No he won't!" Rosamund brushed the crumbs off her fingers and onto her nightgown with an angry gesture. "For one thing, he has a separate compartment. Miss Nordstrom and I share, and then he's got the one next to ours. But all he ever thinks about is business and all the cables and letters and things that he's always getting from foreign places. I could jump straight off the train and Father wouldn't notice! Or he'd only tell me to be a good girl and mind what Miss Nordstrom says."

I could hear an echo of her father's curt, dismissive voice in her tone.

I sighed. When I had come into his life, Holmes had doubted his own ability to be a successful father. Little did he know, I had frequently run across men and women who made him look as though he ought to be writing an advice column on parenting for the London Times.

"I'm sorry," I told Rosamund. "But we'd better get you back to your own compartment before Miss Nordstrom really does start to worry about where you've gone. I'll come with you."

Rosamund's shoulders slumped again, but she clambered down off the bed without argument. "Thank you for the biscuits, anyway."

"You're very welcome," I told her.

A sudden and completely unexpected wave of homesickness washed through me. I had lived most of my life without any real home or family. I'd learned in the past two years that the trouble with having a home was that you could miss it so sharply it was almost physically painful when you were away. I would have given anything to be back in London now, sitting in front of the fire with Jack and engaging in one of our nightly battles to get Becky to stay in bed.

Rosamund was a year or two younger than Becky, and nothing like her to look at. But in that moment, she reminded me a little of her all the same.

Before reaching for the door, I bent down so that my eyes were on a level with hers. "If Miss Nordstrom fusses, we'll tell her that I invited you to come and keep me company for a little while. And whether or not you believe me, I do like you. You're welcome to come and visit me here any time."

26. LUCY

The lights in the train corridor were turned down low as I made my way back to my own compartment after having delivered Rosamund to hers. Thanks to my explanation, Miss Nordstrom's fussing had been kept to a minimum—although she had looked patently incredulous at my thanking Rosamund for the pleasure of her company.

Children, despite all adult opinions to the contrary, weren't stupid, and with a child's unflinching perception, Rosamund had summed up the situation exactly: Miss Nordstrom cared for the little girl solely out of duty, and because she would lose her post if she failed at her job.

The knowledge no doubt made Rosamund act out all the more in consequence.

I was deep enough in thought that I nearly forgot to look where I was going. When a door to one of the compartments on the left opened and the Honourable Richard Mallowe came reeling out, I had to stop short to keep from walking straight into him.

"Hello, there." He peered at me through a clearly alcoholic haze. "Don't believe I've had the pleasure of making your ah-ac-acquai—" He gave up on trying to force his tongue to pronounce the word. "Don't believe that we've met."

He had already seized hold of my hand with one of his hot, dry ones.

"My name is Clarice Earnshaw," I told him.

"Clareesh," he repeated, mangling the word. "Prrrretty name. Pretty girl, too. Not that there's much competition on this train." He snorted, breathing what felt like an entire winery's worth of alcoholic fumes into my face. "You're the only thing worth looking at among all the old fossils on board."

If this was Mr. Mallowe's best effort at seduction, it was a wonder that he had any love affairs at all, much less the dozens to which society newspapers gave him credit.

But young, unmarried, and innocent Miss Clarice Earnshaw wouldn't be expected to make that observation. Nor would she know how to extract herself from Mr. Mallowe's grasp—a task that was becoming increasingly difficult as he leaned forward and tried to put a hand on my waist.

I was itching to stamp hard on his instep, or execute a manoeuvre that would leave him with a sprained or possibly broken wrist. But that would give my cover away.

If Mr. Mallowe wasn't genuinely inebriated, he was a remarkably fine actor. But there was always a chance that this was a test. Or that one of the other train passengers might be watching.

Accordingly, I summoned up a shy smile. "You're too kind. But I really think that I must be going—"

"Oh, don't go yet." Mr. Mallowe tightened his grip on my hand. "We're only just getting acqu-acqu—" he gave up again. "Only just getting to know each other."

I was weighing my options for extracting myself with a minimum of awkwardness—and not feeling especially sanguine about any of them—when I was saved from having to act by another compartment door opening.

It was the door next to mine, which made it the compartment

of the Austrian viscount, the one who was too old and feeble to dine in the restaurant car.

Old, he certainly was. A bald head, much liver-spotted and ringed with a meagre fringe of white hair like a tonsure, protruded out from the compartment like a turtle from its shell. The count's face was quite remarkable in its ugliness: a great jutting beak of a nose, thin lips, and sharp eyes set under shaggy white brows.

He scowled at us, speaking in heavily accented English. "A little quiet, if you please, out there! Some of us require to rest!"

I doubted that Mr. Mallowe would have any concern for Count Styptovich's rest. But he'd startled at the count's sudden appearance, loosening his grip on my hand.

"Good night!" I pushed past Mr. Mallow, opened the door of my own compartment, and swiftly went inside before he had entirely realised what had happened. I snapped the lock behind me, adding the safety chain, then leaned back against the closed door.

The travelling clock I'd already put on the small bedside stand showed the time to be nearly half past nine. Another few hours, and we would be in Munich, and then it would be roughly another two and a half days until we reached Constantinople.

At the moment, those fifty-odd hours seemed to stretch out before me, interminably long.

WEDNESDAY, 13 JULY

27. WATSON

Thirty hours later, in the dark early hours before dawn, I dressed and left my compartment.

Maurice dozed on his chair at the end of the shadowy corridor. He did not see me, I thought. I opened the outer door and stepped onto the steel platform into the rushing night air. The steel ladder was beside me, and I used it to haul myself up to the rooftop.

I needed to get away from the stifling atmosphere of my closed compartment. The false identity I had taken, the oversweet luxury of silken sheets and garments that were not mine, all cloyed my thoughts. I needed to clear my mind. In a few hours we would be in Constantinople and I would face the woman calling herself Jane Griffin, with her beautiful hard features and her false smile. Whatever she had planned would happen, and I would have to respond quickly and decisively. Holmes's life might be at stake, as well as my own. Was she really working with Holmes? Could I trust her?

She had promised that when we met at the station on the morrow it would all be made clear. She thought Holmes would be there. Holmes, she said, would banish my doubts. I had asked what would happen when Clegg and Holmes saw one another. "Likely Holmes will not appear as Holmes," was her reply. "We both know he is a master of disguise."

Fruitless conversations.

Speculations, Holmes would have said.

So here I was, crouched on a rooftop of a railway carriage, catching my breath in the July heat. I clutched the bars of the steel ladder as the train rattled its way to the east and the new day. This morning would mark our arrival in Constantinople, and I would begin the end of a game to which I knew none of the rules and not even all the players.

We were steaming along the shore of what my guidebook map had proclaimed the Sea of Marmara. Seven cars ahead of where I perched, a crescent moon cast its light onto surrounding clouds, partially obscured by the swirl of lignite smoke from the locomotive. The dawn would begin from that direction. Alongside the train I could see shadows of ancient ruins, grim heaps of stone walls that once had been buildings of importance, filled with lives and longings. The minaret tower of a small abandoned mosque seemed to flare up and then fall away as we passed it by, lit by a flash of lightning. I wondered if a storm was coming. I wondered if there would be a break in the oppressive heat.

Shoot the Torrance woman, Sonnebourne had said, and then pushed a photograph across the desk.

Torrance was never my husband, Jane Griffin had said.

And then I knew. Or felt certain that I knew.

Deduction, not speculation. Deduction from facts! I whispered the words to myself. I tried to arrange the facts logically, but I was distracted by the huge wave of relief and triumph that swept through me. I very nearly sprang to my feet, though that would have been a disastrous move to make upon the roof of a swaying, speeding train. *Steady on, Watson*, I told myself. *Pride goeth before a fall.*

I tried once more to arrange the facts into the chain of logic. But I could not.

Still, I *knew*.

I looked ahead, where I thought I saw a bluish tint above the black horizon. Dawn and Constantinople, the Torrance woman, and Clegg awaited me. And possibly Holmes.

But what would I do about it?

Then from behind and below me came Clegg's voice, in his mock-Cockney accent. "Out for a breath of fresh air, are we, Milord?"

"That's quite correct, Roland," I said. For some reason I felt jauntier now than since my journey had begun.

"Thought so, Milord. Mind your step on the way down, Milord."

I returned to my compartment, and packed.

28. WATSON

The sun had been up for nearly an hour when the train arrived in Constantinople. I stepped down from the railway carriage, dazzled by the bright morning sun, so much more powerful than what I was accustomed to in London. The station was newly built in what appeared to be golden sandstone, on such a grand scale that it might have been a cathedral. Along the horizon I could see minaret spires far taller than the one I had observed during the night. The air was cleaner than in London or Paris. The crowd waiting at the station seemed less impatient than those I had seen in European cities, though possibly that was due to the limitations of my own perception.

I watched Maurice stepping down with my luggage, two gleaming and expensive leather suitcases that John H. Watson, M.D, would never have dreamed of purchasing. He loaded them onto a cart. I took several bills from the packet I still retained and passed them over to Maurice. He thanked me and whistled up a platform attendant for my luggage cart.

On the platform up ahead Jane Griffin stood beside the next car, waiting for her own luggage. She waved at me and gestured towards the station.

"She has the finest car," Maurice said. "The one farthest from the engine noise and smoke. Have you travelled with her and the gentleman before, monsieur Milord?" he asked.

"Gentleman?"

"The one in third-class carriage?" He stroked his hand above his head to mime a short haircut.

"No. My first time."

"You should take care, Milord. I have seen them before with other people. But I have never seen those other people return."

"They make people disappear," I said.

"As long as you are aware, Milord."

I caught up with Jane Griffin. I turned and saw Clegg, striding forward, carrying his own suitcase.

"Poor fellow," Jane Griffin said. "Doomed to third-class travel." We watched him. He stopped alongside the last car, set down his suitcase, and knelt to tie his shoe. A few moments after that he was with us.

"We'll all go together to the hotel, shall we?" said Jane Griffin.

"Jolly fun," said Clegg.

* * *

We rode in an open landau carriage, pulled by two white horses, bearing the insignia of the Wagons-Lits company. "The Orient Express company owns the hotel," Jane Griffin said. "It's quite pleasant, actually."

"How long will we be staying?"

"That depends," she said.

We approached a bridge across a wide waterway. I tried to recall the images from the map I had looked at.

"We are crossing the Bosporus," Jane Griffin said. "If you look to your right, at the top of the hill, you can see Topkapi Palace. The sultan and the seat of government are there. I mention it because what happens at Topkapi will determine how long we stay here."

"Days, weeks?" I said.

"It depends on progress. If agreement is reached, then to-morrow. If no agreement, then Friday. Both sides will of course claim progress and congratulate each other. But Friday is the last day possible. They have been here nearly a month."

"What are they doing?"

"You don't need to know."

"Oh, it's no great secret" Clegg said. "Well, as between our-selves, it isn't. To the public, of course, it is a secret. Quite an important one."

I looked at him expectantly. "Go on."

"Sorry," Clegg said. "Must leave you now. Some business to attend to." He vaulted out of the landau, leaving his suitcase. "Check me in to the hotel, will you?"

She nodded. He vanished into a crowd of pedestrians, cart-drivers, vendors, oxen, donkey-carts, and women carrying bas-kets. All seemed in a hurry.

"A good place to disappear," she said.

We rode in silence.

"It goes back ten years," Jane Griffin said. "The European powers signed a treaty declaring the Suez Canal to be neutral. But our people—"

"Sonnebourne?"

She smiled. "Not Sonnebourne's people. I ought to have been clear on that point. England voiced official reservations to the treaty. The government agrees that ships can pass through, but will not allow the army to be restricted in keeping the area safe."

"Since we control Egypt."

"And France doesn't support those reservations. Pure pop-pycock, diplomatically speaking. England paid France, after all, for its ownership in the canal. But they say the restriction weakens the treaty."

"Posturing."

"Quite, but public official disagreement is bad. So the powers-that-be are in Topkapi Palace, trying to work out some face-saving declaration. It goes on and on."

"Ten years."

"And counting."

"Where does Sonnebourne come in?"

"The French official is here. As is England's negotiating fellow. Lord Lansdowne."

I must have changed my expression, for Jane Griffin looked at me sharply. "You know Lord Lansdowne?"

"I've met him, yes."

Saved his life, I might have added. *Twice.* But I kept that to myself. I asked, "He's the target?"

"No, not him. The Frenchman is the target. The Sonnebourne organization is being paid to kill the Frenchman."

"And Sonnebourne is paying you to do that."

She shrugged. "He'll be very, very disappointed when I don't."

* * *

A suite on an upper floor of the Pera Palace hotel awaited me. Jane Griffin had the suite next door. We rode up in the electric lift together. The platform was enclosed with ornamental wrought-iron bars that resembled a cage. The bellman let us into our rooms, Miss Griffin first. "You each have your own balcony," he said. "The view of the Golden Horn is a famous one. Quite exceptional."

"I've seen it," she said.

"The Wagons-Lits company has a tour organised," he said. "Complimentary for new arrivals who are guests of the hotel. Do either of you wish to take it?"

I decided to test whether Jane Griffin would want to keep a leash on me. "I will go," I said.

"You do that, Milord," she said. "I have other plans."

So, I toured Constantinople with several other fellow passengers I recognised from the train. We saw remnants of past civilizations that had occupied the city. Obelisk towers from the Egyptians. A Roman hippodrome, where chariot races had once been held for the amusement of the masses. Stunning Christian mosaics in a Byzantine cathedral. An impossibly diverse labyrinth of colourful shops, all under one roof at the Grand Bazaar.

When I returned, dazed and bedazzled, later that afternoon there was a message for me at the desk. "Supper at 8 tomorrow. JG."

I gave a sigh of relief. I was free until the end of the day tomorrow. Thursday.

On an impulse I asked the clerk if Mr. Sherlock Holmes had registered at the hotel. The answer was a very polite, "No, Milord."

Then the clerk nodded towards the adjoining space, where soaring walls and huge coloured-glass ceiling domes created the atmosphere of a great cathedral. "Afternoon tea is served until six, Milord. British style, very fine indeed. Would you care to partake?"

Seize the moment, Holmes would have told me.

"Indeed," I said.

THURSDAY, JULY 14

29. WATSON

Rose petals were strewn on our table in the Pera Palace dining room. Above them were gilded dishes of apricots, skewered meat, yoghurt, and flat bread. Jane Griffin sat across from me, her dark eyes searching mine.

"Enjoying Constantinople, Milord?"

I shrugged. "News of the treaty?"

"Nothing. But tomorrow is the last day. They'll be departing, agreement or no. Tomorrow afternoon will be our moment."

She took a telegram from her purse and handed it to me. It was dated from Sofia Railway station at four o'clock and read:

JANE GRIFFIN, PERA PALACE.
ARRIVE FRIDAY MORNING STOP
SECOND A IDENTIFIED STOP
MUST PREVENT STOP
WILL SEND PHOTOGRAPH STOP SH END

" 'SH' is 'Sherlock Holmes,' of course," she said.

"And 'second A' means a second assassin," I said.

"Do you read it that way? After all, you know him better than I do."

"Since the first assassin is ..."

She nodded. "Though I've promised I won't."

"Now, as to 'must prevent,' " I said. "How will we stop him— or her?"

"I'm going to be busy with Clegg."

"Busy?"

"Killing him. Since he's been ordered to frame you."

"You mentioned that at dinner," I said.

"So, I'm afraid stopping the other fellow ..." she let her voice trail off.

"Is up to me," I said.

"That's how I read it."

30. LUCY

My eyes snapped open, and I lay a moment in the darkness, uncertain of what had awakened me. This was the second night of our journey. We had passed through Vienna and Budapest, and were now on the final leg of the journey that would take us through Bucharest and from there to Constantinople.

The day had passed as slowly as I had foreseen. I had sat with Lady Danville for all of the meals served in the restaurant car—which at least had the benefit of keeping Richard Mallowe away. Lady Danville had undertaken to convince him of the error of his wicked ways, causing him to avoid her like the proverbial plague.

Count Styptovich had kept to his room, but Father Jerome, the Catholic Priest, had made an appearance in the dining car at luncheon. I had spent most of the afternoon playing cards with Rosamund—with Miss Nordstrom periodically interrupting to tell a scowling Rosamund that she needed to eat her vegetables or do her lessons or comb her hair.

After dinner, I had gone to bed early. And now the communicating door between my compartment and Count Styptovich's was slowly opening. That was the sound that had awakened me—the snick of the latch as it was raised from the other side.

I let out a breath, relaxing back against the pillows. "It's all right." I kept my voice low, mindful that one of the attendants or other passengers might be passing by in the corridor outside. "I'm already awake."

The door swung inwards and Count Styptovich's domed bald head and beaky nose were revealed in the opening.

"I would have come earlier," Sherlock Holmes said. "But I wished to give the sedative that I slipped into the attendant's water earlier tonight time to take effect."

I blinked. No matter how prepared I thought I was for Holmes, he still managed to catch me off guard. "You drugged our conductor?"

"Naturally." Holmes came the rest of the way into the room, shutting the door behind him. "A minor dose only. He will wake in an hour or two, believing merely that he fell asleep while on duty. But as you have no doubt observed, his chair is at the end of the carriage, making it impossible to explore the rest of the train without his being aware."

Since Holmes had not attempted to contact me last night, I had been prepared for him to make an appearance tonight and had gone to sleep fully dressed. The time on my bedside clock now read a quarter past three in the morning.

I pushed back the eiderdown coverlet and stood up, eyeing Holmes' Count Styptovich disguise with fascination.

"Aren't you worried that nose will melt straight off your face in this hot weather? I've never seen you use quite so much putty before."

"An overwhelmingly distinguishing feature for observers to focus on was necessary. Otherwise someone might be liable to notice that there are similarities in appearance between the Austrian viscount and Father Jerome."

I had already recognised Holmes in both personas. "Hence the Count's infirmity that requires him to keep mostly to his compartment. It must have been quite a feat to manage to board the train twice, though, as two different people."

"Less so than you might think." Holmes crossed to the door, opened in a crack, and peered cautiously out into the corridor outside. "The Wagons-Lits attendants, while conscientious in their duties, have a narrow focus of attention that seldom observes details beyond the execution of those same duties. Ah." He drew back, lowering his voice still more. "Our conductor is safely asleep, and there is no one else about. I believe now would be an opportune time for us to make our exit. We will proceed one at a time. If anyone happens to catch sight of one or the other of us, they will assume that we are merely seeking the wash room or stretching our legs."

Holmes exited first, making his way down the corridor with the bent, hunched-over walk of an elderly and infirm man.

I waited until he had reached the door that led into the next carriage, then followed, holding my breath I stepped quickly down the aisle.

True to Holmes' word, our attendant was slumped over in his chair, snoring gently. I edged my way past him, then followed Holmes into the next carriage, which proved to be the gentlemen's smoking lounge, and thankfully deserted at this late hour of the night.

"What is our aim?" I murmured to Holmes, when I had caught up to him.

"I thought an examination of the baggage cars might prove fruitful. At a minimum, it might provide some clue as to whether any of our fellow passengers are not what they seem."

Holmes, like Rosamund, had provided himself with a train attendant's pass key, and now used it to unlock the doors that lay between us and the first of the train's two baggage cars. Save for the light of the corridor lamps behind us, the baggage car was entirely in darkness. But after entering and closing the door, Holmes drew something out from the pocket of his dressing gown and switched it on, causing light to spill from a glass bulb.

"What is that?"

The device resembled a cross between a candle stick and the lamps that were mounted on carriages for driving at night.

"A new invention. American in origin," Holmes said. "Sold by the United States Battery Company. Battery powered, and called the O.T. Bugg Friendly Beacon Electric Candle, in honour of its inventor, Owen T. Bugg, Jr." He glanced at the small lantern with appreciation. "I owe Mr. Bugg a debt. I had thought of inventing something along these lines myself, but he has saved me the trouble. Now, let us not tarry any longer. Time is getting on."

The baggage compartment was crammed with trunks, crates, and suitcases of every description, as one might expect. Those who could afford passage on the Orient Express were accustomed to taking all of their worldly comforts with them when they travelled.

With the aid of the lock-picks that Holmes had also brought, we unlocked trunks and valises and made rapid inspections of their contents. We found nothing, save that Mr. Mallowe's taste in literature ran to some decidedly off-colour magazines, and that the Italian wine merchants had bought cases of cigars while in Paris.

When an hour had passed without any more productive discoveries, I was beginning to feel uneasy prickles at the back of my neck. Holmes had ensured that our Wagons-Lits conductor would be asleep, but he couldn't have drugged every attendant aboard the train. What were the odds that one of the train passengers would suddenly discover the need for an item in one of their stowed-away suitcases, and send off the attendant to fetch it?

Holmes' sharply indrawn breath cut off my thought, and turning, I found him kneeling in front of a plain, unlabelled wooden crate with a few tufts of packing straw poking out through the slats at the top.

"What is it?" I asked.

Holmes inhaled again, slowly, his nose bent to the crate. "Tell me if you smell anything from this crate here."

The baggage car wasn't as well insulated as the others, and at the moment, I couldn't imagine a scent strong enough to overpower the smell of smoke and hot oil from the train's engine. But I complied, bending to draw in a breath next to the wooden container.

My eyes widened. "Gunpowder?"

"So I thought, as well. Come." There was a metal bar on the floor that the train attendants probably used for levering heavy baggage onto and off of the train. Holmes took it up and used it to pry up the nails that held the crate closed. Then he raised his electric candle.

I had to bite my lip as the straw-packed contents of the shipping container became clear.

"Guns."

There were at least a dozen of them, not just revolvers, but rifles, as well, with boxes of ammunition. And beneath those were several round devices that were unpleasantly familiar.

"Plate bombs?" I asked Holmes.

"Indeed."

One of the same devices that had nearly killed Flynn a few days before. It was seldom that I saw Holmes caught off guard by a development in an investigation, but for the moment shock tightened his features. Then his mouth settled into a grim line.

"The Suez Canal lies in a notoriously volatile part of the world, with tensions running high between the native Egyptians and the Ottomans, who nominally control the region. And although the Suez has been declared neutral territory, it remains a potential powder keg which a single ignited match could cause to explode."

"The potential lighted match being these weapons?"

"As you say. The Urabi Revolt of the early 1880's led to widespread violence and rioting across Egypt that cost the lives of hundreds of innocents. If someone today were to transport these weapons to Egypt, then incite the populace to violence—"

"And if British security was to let these weapons proceed there from Constantinople, having been distracted by assassination of one of the French officials at the treaty talks—"

Holmes and I both looked down at the crated rifles and hand guns in their bed of straw. I spoke the thought that was in both our minds. "This isn't just an assassination we're trying to prevent," I said. "It's a potential war."

31. LUCY

"Why would Lord Sonnebourne want to incite violence in Egypt?"

We were back in Holmes'—or rather Count Styptovich's—compartment, having returned to our own railway carriage just as the drugged attendant was beginning to stir.

I was perched on the edge of the bunk. Holmes was sitting cross-legged on the floor, in as close an approximation of his Baker Street nest of cushions as the pillows from the bed could form. From the tension in the line of his jaw, I thought he would be clamping a lit pipe between his teeth were it not for his role of a supposedly frail elderly gentleman whose lungs would not withstand thick tobacco smoke.

His eyes were closed, and he answered me without opening them. "What Lord Sonnebourne's personal interest is, we cannot be certain. But I am reminded of a certain European power with which we have tangled before—one bent on dominating the continent and doing everything in its power to thwart Britain."

"You're speaking of Germany."

"Indeed."

"So our working theory is that Sonnebourne is in the pay of the Kaiser?"

"The theory requires proof. But it seems at present the most plausible explanation to fit the facts of the case. Whether Sonnebourne feels any actual allegiance to Kaiser Wilhelm, or whether he simply accepts payment in the way he does from his stolen identity clients remains to be seen."

I looked at the clock. In just a few short hours, we would reach Constantinople. "What are we to do about the weapons? Should we report them to a railway official?"

"That would involve an explanation of how two supposedly ordinary passengers came to be prying open crates in a sealed and locked baggage compartment—as well as inevitable questions as to why we are travelling under false identity papers. All of which would cause significant delays."

"And we need to find Watson as soon as possible."

Holmes nodded. "Besides, we took the precaution of confiscating the ammunition from both the revolvers and the rifles."

The bullets were now residing in Count Styptovich's suitcase, and without them or a replacement supply of ammunition, the weapons would be useless.

"We must assume, though, that this shipment was merely one of many," Holmes went on. "Which leads us to another likely if unfavourable possibility: that at least one if not more of the train's employees are also in the Kaiser's pay."

He was right, and it was another reason to keep silent about our discovery: if we reported the weapons to the wrong person, we would be exposing our own real identities to exactly those individuals most interested in making sure that we never stepped off the Orient Express alive.

"I suggest that you return to your own compartment and get what rest you can before our arrival," Holmes said. "I shall do the same. And when we arrive in Constantinople, we can proceed with our endeavour to find Watson, and report the shipment of weapons to Lord Lansdown and the other officials at the summit."

"Not all of whom may be honest, either. The assassin could be among those at the talks."

"True." Holmes's eyes were closed again. "But there are times in an investigation where one's best strategy is to rustle the bushes in the manner of the beaters on a duck hunt—and see what manner of creature flies out."

FRIDAY, JULY 15

32. LUCY

Against all odds, I slept for an hour or two after regaining my own compartment. When I had woken and dressed, the attendant brought me hot coffee and the news that the train was running a few minutes behind schedule, but would nevertheless reach Constantinople in half an hour's time.

I packed my suitcase, then sat down by the window, wishing that I could speak with Holmes again. But especially in daylight hours it was safer that Clarice Earnshaw and Count Styptovich have no contact whatsoever with one another.

A tap at the door made me startle, my heart quickening. But the knocker was only Miss Nordstrom, her brows pinched together in an anxious frown.

"Is Rosamund here with you?"

"No, I've not seen her all morning."

"It's very naughty of her. I can't find her anywhere." Despite my assertion, Miss Nordstrom peered into my compartment as though she suspected Rosamund of hiding under the bed. "She must have run off and hidden the way she does, but we'll be arriving soon, and I don't know what to do!" Miss Nordstrom's thin hands twisted together. "Her father will be so angry!"

I privately thought that in order for Mr. Anstruther to be angry over Rosamund's disappearance, he would first have to notice that she was gone.

But out loud all I said was, "Well, she must be somewhere

on the train, and she'll have to come out when we get to Constantinople. I wouldn't worry."

Miss Nordstrom didn't look entirely reassured, but she did turn to leave, murmuring, "Oh dear, oh dear," as she hurried off down the corridor.

* * *

Müşir Ahmet Paşa Station in Constantinople was a new construction, built in a style that fused the gothic with the oriental. Twin clock towers flanked the domed central building, which was ornamented with a stained-glass window that echoed the style of the famous Rose Window of Notre Dame.

Miss Nordstrom was still wringing her hands and looking worried as I stepped down onto the train platform.

"Has Rosamund not been found yet?" For the first time, I felt a prick of worry. But then, Rosamund could hardly have jumped off the train. "Have you checked the empty compartments?" I asked.

Miss Nordstrom nodded tearfully. "The conductors are searching now, but so far she's nowhere to be found! Oh, do please be careful with that!" she added.

One of the porters had been struggling to load her own and Rosamund's luggage onto a baggage cart, and had fumbled with one of the trunks, causing it to slip partway to the ground.

"Be careful!" Miss Nordstrom bleated again. "All of Rosamund's bottles of strengthening tonic are inside there, and I don't want them broken!"

Mr. Anstruther stood a little off to one side, tapping his foot and scowling down at his pocket watch, which he held open in one hand.

"This really is most inconvenient. Most inconvenient indeed. I have an urgent appointment across the city in three quarters of an hour that cannot possibly be postponed." He looked up. "Miss Nordstrom, there is nothing to be done but for you to remain here until Rosamund is found. Then bring her to the hotel. The Pera Palace is the name. A suite of rooms has already been engaged for us, you need only ask at the front desk."

"Yes, Mr. Anstruther. Of course, I'll wait here just as you say. I can't think what the child can have been thinking of, it's so naughty of her." Miss Nordstrom blinked pale lashes and twisted her hands together again. "I hope you don't think I've been in any way remiss in my duties, Mr. Anstruther. I did try to look after her and to keep an eye on her at all times, but she's so quick—"

"Not at all. I'm sure you did your best." Mr. Anstruther cut short his employees' anxious twittering with a curt nod. "I will see you back at the hotel this evening." He started to swing round, but then his eye fell on me. "I understand that you, ah, befriended my daughter on the journey." He cleared his throat, then added, "I'm most grateful," in a gruff tone before striding off.

I was left staring after him in surprise as he vanished into the crowd of departing passengers and porters wheeling carts of luggage.

A sharp jab to my ankle brought me back to myself, coupled with the sound of a violent fit of sneezing.

Holmes, in the persona of Count Styptovich, had just jabbed me with his walking stick and blown his nose practically in my ear as he hobbled by. A salutary reminder that we didn't have time to spare, any more than Mr. Anstruther did.

I turned back to Miss Nordstrom. "I hope Rosamund decides to be found soon," I told her. "Maybe I'll see the two of you at the hotel. I'm staying at the Pera Palace, as well."

33. WATSON

It was just after noon Friday when I heard a knock at the door of my room. Jane Griffin's voice. "Lord Harwell?"

I was ready for her, wearing Harwell's finest black silk suit with a dove-grey waistcoat. She wore a long-sleeved dress of dove-grey silk and a straw hat dyed to match. She gave me an appraising look.

"We appear well together."

"Perhaps we should have a photograph taken."

"Another time," she said. "You need to go to the ceremony. I've had a message from Holmes."

"Where is he?"

"I don't know." She withdrew a brown envelope from her purse. "He sent this photograph. And a name."

From the envelope she withdrew a photograph of a dignified, middle-aged man with sleek dark hair and a walrus moustache. Two words were affixed with paste, each clipped from a newspaper. "The assassin."

I studied the photograph, trying to imagine what the man would look like when seen from behind. Was it the same man I had seen across from Sonnebourne a week ago? I could not tell.

"Go and take care of this man," she said. "His name is Anstruther. He will be in the crowd somewhere, within sight of the platform where the departure ceremony will be held. Leave now. Be in place early. The ceremony starts in an hour. But watch out for Clegg. His job is to oversee the shooting and see that you are blamed."

"How will he do that?"

"I don't know. But I'll be watching him, and when he makes his move, I will kill him."

"I hope you know what you're doing."

"It's the one thing I do well," she said. "Now you must leave. When you have stopped the assassin, find Holmes. He will be somewhere in the crowd."

"What about you?"

"I told you on the train. I'll come back here for the money. I'll be leaving here just after the Orient Express departs. At two."

"I won't see you again?"

"Only if you decide to come with me."

"It's a thought," I said.

"I'll walk you to the staircase."

She did. She watched me walk down the wide marble steps. I turned at the first landing, and she was still watching. I waved, nodded, and continued down to the lobby.

Then I rode the lift back upstairs. On the fourth floor I let myself into the Harwell room with my key. Then I climbed out the window, and then over my terrace wall.

I stood on the ledge for a moment. Below me was the Golden Horn harbour, but I did not take time to appreciate the view. I edged my way along the narrow stone surface to the window of Jane Griffin's suite.

The window was open.

34. LUCY

"You would like tea, sir, while you are waiting?" the hotel clerk asked for the fourth time.

Holmes and I were standing at the front desk in the ornate lobby of the Pera Palace.

Outside, the city streets were hot and dusty, with bright clumps of pink and purple bougainvillea growing from the peeling plaster walls. The interior of the hotel, though, was cool and luxurious. Polished marble columns supported the vaulted ceiling. Curtains of red velvet hung at the windows, and the lobby benches and chairs were upholstered in a matching red and gold brocade.

Holmes had discarded his Count Styptovich disguise and now appeared as himself—and was currently looking as though he were restraining the urge to vault across the desk between us and strangle the clerk with his bare hands.

"I would not like tea. All I wish is for you to examine your records and tell me whether you currently have a room occupied by Gerald, Lord Harwell."

"Or Dr. John H. Watson," I added.

Holmes glanced at me, and I said, in an undertone, "If he's not a prisoner, there's always a chance that he might have engaged the room under his own name, isn't there?"

The clerk bobbed his head. "Yes, sir, yes, Madame. Perfectly, perfectly."

He had been persuaded by Mycroft's official-looking documents that he was duty-bounded to show us the hotel's guest books. Not that he would have required much in the way of persuading in any case. Thin and anxious-looking, he swallowed nervously as he flipped open the heavy leather-bound volume that contained the hotel's records. "I just thought that perhaps a cup of tea while you wait—"

At Holmes' look, he abandoned the sentence, swallowed again, and began to run his finger down the long column of names. "Ah yes. Here it is. A room checked out two days ago to Gerald, Lord Harwell. Just as you say." He beamed at us. "Room number 506."

"Thank you."

Holmes turned away. "We can go to the room—" he started to say.

"Sir! A moment only—"

Holmes swung back around and the clerk flinched at the intensity of his glare. "Well?" Holmes demanded.

"It is only—the young lady did mention a Dr. Watson, did she not, sir? A Dr. John Watson?"

"Yes?"

"Well, it is just that we have a room checked out under that name, as well," the clerk faltered. "You see?" He turned the leather guest book around so that we could look.

The entry had been made on the most recent page. At the bottom were Holmes's and my names with room numbers beside them—although I doubted that we would get the chance to ever occupy those rooms. Mr. Anstruther had signed the registry just above us, for a suite of rooms on the hotel's second floor.

And a few lines above that was the entry that the desk clerk had pointed to: "John H. Watson, M.D. Room number 424."

35. WATSON

The woman calling herself Jane Griffin sat at her dressing table, as though putting on makeup before her mirror. For a moment I feared she had seen my reflection. But as I waited, frozen, she bent down, reached beneath the dressing table, and lifted up a black leather valise that very much resembled my own medical bag. This was different, however; two brass clasps sat on either end of the central spine rather than the single one I was accustomed to opening.

She snapped open the clasps, one at a time, and then, turning to the bed behind her, lifted the open valise and turned it upside down.

Packets of bank notes spilled across the white fabric coverlet. She quickly arranged the packets into five rows and five columns. Then she carefully repackaged them into the valise. Leaving it open on the bed, she opened a drawer in her dressing table and withdrew a shining silver pistol. She clicked it open, examined the cartridges inside, and then clicked it shut before carefully tucking it into the valise. She closed both clasps and tucked the valise behind the bolster pillow at the head of the bed, pulling up the coverlet.

Then came a knock from the door to her sitting room. As she went to answer it, I quietly swung my leg over the window sill and stood, holding my breath. Another knock came. I tiptoed on the carpet to the connecting door, where I could see into the sitting room through the crack between the edge of the connecting door and its frame.

The woman opened the door and stepped back. A man entered.

For a moment his back was towards me, and I recognised his sleek black hair. The assassin.

But then he turned, and I saw his face.

Clegg.

But what did that mean?

"Well?" the woman asked.

"Armed and timer set. Where's my money?"

"Somewhere safe, until I see results."

She nodded towards the door and he opened it, stepped aside, and held it open as she left the room. He followed and said, "I'm not letting you out of my sight."

The door closed behind them.

I made my way back to Harwell's room, opened the door slowly, and waited until I heard the chain-like clang of the lift door shutting. Then I made my way down the wide marble staircase that surrounded the lift, taking care to always remain far enough above the cage to avoid being visible through the openings between the wrought iron bars.

From the stairway I watched them descend to the lobby, exit the lift, and walk together through the doors to the street. Then an ox-cart passed, and the huge brown beasts blocked my view. I could not see which direction they went.

By the time I reached the street, they were out of my sight.

36. LUCY

Holmes rapped on the door of room 506, waited, and then receiving no reply, extracted his bunch of lock picks. We were beginning with the room checked out to Lord Harwell, for the simple reason that the corridor outside of it was currently empty, while the hallway outside room 424 was occupied by a large party of lady tourists who were assembling to take a walking tour of the city.

A few quick twists of the picks, and the door of room 506 swung open. I held my breath, but a quick glance was enough to tell that the room was empty. We made a rapid search all the same, checking the ornate four-poster bed and the big mahogany wardrobe.

"The hotel staff have done an admirably thorough job with this morning's cleaning," Holmes said when we had finished. "Which in this case is unfortunate for our purposes. However, it is worth observing that the clothes in the wardrobe, while not belonging to Watson, are nevertheless custom tailored to a man of his measurements."

"There's nothing to show where he is now, though. Or if he has been staying here, why he should have booked a second room under his real name." I surveyed the room one final time, frustration mingled with worry gnawing at me. "Shall we go and look through the second room now? Unless you want to leave some sort of message for Watson here, in case he does return?"

Holmes considered. "We cannot risk anything too obvious, in case Watson is not the one to next enter this room after all. However—"

He took two matches from the hotel's complimentary book, crossed them, and placed them on the table beside the bed.

"Now come. Let us see what the room of John H. Watson, MD, can tell us."

* * *

It would have been too much to expect that Watson would be in room 424, safe and sound. But a part of me must have entertained the slight hope for it all the same, because my heart dropped when we found the room as empty as the one on the floor above.

This room, though, had not been cleaned. The bed was unmade, and the air was stale with the odour of cigarette smoke.

"The hotel staff must have been given directions not to tidy up this morning," I said as we stood side by side in the doorway.

"Which leads one to the question of why—and who gave the order for the place to remain untouched."

A nearly empty bottle of whiskey and a tumbler, still half-full of amber brown liquid, sat on the table beside the bed.

"Whoever has occupied this room, we may assume that he now has a headache of considerable proportions," Holmes went on. "If he indeed emptied the better part of that bottle of whiskey into his interior last night."

As he spoke, he crossed to the table and picked the glass up carefully by its rim. "One set of fingerprints only." He held it up to the light streaming in through the uncurtained window, then gave a sharp exclamation. "These are Watson's fingermarks."

"You're sure?"

"I know them as well as I know my own." Holmes' lips tightened at the edges. "The glass, though. It's not one of the hotel's."

"You're right." The sick, uneasy feeling that had been with me all morning settled in a cold lump directly under my rib cage. "That's one of the glasses that they use on the Orient Express train. Someone took a glass that Uncle John had used on the train so that his fingerprints would be on it, then carefully brought it off the train and planted it here to make it look as though he'd drunk an entire bottle of whiskey last night. Why?"

"I am fairly certain that neither one of us is going to like the answer to that question," Holmes said.

"What's this?" I had caught sight of a small leather-covered book lying half under the bed, as though someone had accidentally knocked it off the night table. "It looks like a diary."

Opening the volume, I quickly scanned the words that had been scrawled across the first page.

"May God forgive me for what I am about to do," I read out loud. "Murder is indeed a great sin. But when ordered by one's own crown and country, can it really be accounted as any different from the lives a soldier takes while on the battlefield of war?"

I raised my eyes to Holmes. "What is this? The handwriting is quite a good imitation of Watson's. Good enough that it might even fool an expert."

Holmes came to look over my shoulder as I turned the page.

"I continue to have misgivings over the crime I am to commit. But I have given my word as a gentleman, and I cannot withdraw now. The

ceremony of departure, with a joint announcement to the Press to be made between the French delegation and Lord Lansdowne is scheduled for this afternoon, and I must be there to carry out my assigned task. Besides, I must admit that the money will be most welcome—"

"This is absurd," I interrupted. "Handwriting or not, no one who knows Watson would ever believe him capable of writing such drivel."

"That, unfortunately, is precisely the point." Holmes' voice was granite-hard, his expression stony. He was monumentally angry, perhaps more furious than I had ever seen him. "No one in this region of the world—save for ourselves and Lord Lansdowne—does know Watson personally. No one in a position of official power in this country is likely to quibble with his being made into a ready scapegoat."

"A scapegoat for what, exactly—" I broke off as the pieces in my mind arranged themselves into a single, horrifyingly coherent picture. "The assassination Watson tried to warn us about in his telegram. And this diary mentions the departure ceremony to be held this afternoon. The French official is going to be assassinated, and the blame fixed on Watson."

"Destroy those pages," Holmes said. He was already in motion, racing for the door.

37. WATSON

I walked quickly down the hill from the Pera Palace. At the peak of the arch crossing the waterway I stopped to get my bearings. Ahead of me and below, crowds milled aimlessly around the railway station. Neither Clegg or Jane Griffin appeared among them. I waited, scanning the moving hats and coats, looking for those two faces. I noticed officials organising one section of the crowd, creating a passageway wide enough for a carriage to come through.

Then just at my side a man bustled past, in a hurry to get wherever he was going. For a moment I stood motionless. Then the man, realising he had jostled me, I supposed, turned and tipped his hat. I saw his face. Dark hair and a dark walrus moustache.

The man in the photograph? Anstruther?

I could not be certain.

But I could not just let him go either. I followed, resolving to keep him in my sight. And stay close. Because if he made an assassin's move, I would have to stop him.

38. LUCY

The plaza outside of the Müşir Ahmet Paşa Station was crowded with newspaper reporters and photographers, as well as taxi drivers, train passengers, and merchants doing business from the backs of small grey donkeys. Constantinople vendors apparently sold everything from strings of brightly coloured enamel beads to flowers to fruit and spices—and seemed to feel that the louder they conducted their business the better.

One vendor thrust a circular blue glass ornament at me as Holmes and I pushed our way through the crowd. "Lucky charm, Miss? Guaranteed protection from the evil eye!"

I was almost desperate enough to wish I could believe in a good luck charm, but I shook my head and kept moving through the crowds. A podium had been set up at one end of the plaza, and although we were some distance away I could make out the figure of Lord Lansdowne, distinctive in his high black top hat among the other men on the platform.

"Watson won't be alone," Holmes said beside me. He had to raise his voice to be heard over the noise of the crowd. "They'll try to manipulate him into a position from which he might be supposed to have made the fatal shot."

Which meant that he had to be reasonably near the podium, otherwise the newspaper reporters and other bystanders would get in the way.

"What's their plan for afterwards, though? Even if they shoot the French official and put the gun into Watson's hand, he'll fight back—and be able to give an account of himself to the authorities."

"They won't leave him alive." Holmes' face was tight with frustration as he, too, ran his eyes across the assembled people. "They'll make it appear as though he committed the assassination, then took his own life in a fit of remorse, unable to live with the guilt."

Still moving forwards, I scanned the plaza again, then froze.

"There!" I pointed to a spot at the left of the podium, where a face I recognised had at long last caught my eye.

Watson wasn't looking in our direction, and I felt the knot of anxiety clench a few degrees tighter around my heart.

"Do we dare call out to him?" I asked Holmes.

My quick scan hadn't revealed any bystanders obviously keeping watch on Watson, but there must be one—or even more than one. If they knew we were here, they might decide to shoot Watson here and now, before we could intervene.

At the periphery of my attention, I was aware of Lord Lansdowne and another man on the podium standing together and shaking hands, holding the pose.

Newspaper photographers' flash trays ignited and shone brilliantly for a few moments, in a cacophony of tiny pops that sounded to my stretched nerves like a dozen explosions.

If the assassination was to take place, it would have to be soon—any second—while all eyes were on the podium and the ceremony was about to draw to a close.

I was still desperately searching the crowd, hoping to spot whoever was pulling the strings of the assassination attempt, when I realised that standing a little behind Watson was a second figure I knew.

Mr. Anstruther was staring straight ahead, and his face had

the set, despairing look of a soldier marching into a battle he knows he won't survive.

As I watched, he started to reach for the inner pocket of his overcoat.

"Uncle John!"

By some miracle—for I doubted he could actually have heard me—Watson's eyes connected with mine.

"Behind you!" I still doubted he could hear what I said, but I shouted and pointed, hoping he would read my lips. "Behind!"

Watson spun, saw the gun in Mr. Anstruther's hand, and succeeded in tackling him, dragging them both to the ground just as a shot rang out above the noise of the crowd. Another shot rang out. Then another. The crowd scattered in panic.

Holmes was running towards them, but I clutched at his arm.

"Try to keep Mr. Anstruther alive if you possibly can!" I had to keep shouting to be heard above the voices that had changed to terrified screams, and I almost lost my footing as people and donkeys all around us started to run and crash into one another in fear. "He's not acting by choice, he's being blackmailed. Probably he's been blackmailed into being a part of Lord Sonnebourne's organisation!"

For the second time in the course of this investigation, I saw Sherlock Holmes caught off guard.

His brows pinched together. "Where are you going?"

I couldn't see Watson or Mr. Anstruther at all anymore, they were likely still struggling on the ground. I just had to hope desperately that Watson would survive. At least there had been no more shots.

"I have to get back to the Pera Palace hotel," I shouted. "As fast as I can!"

39. WATSON

The dark-haired assassin waved his gun as we struggled for control, but he fired no more shots. He was older than I, and less strong. I knocked him to his knees. The crowd shrank back. I crouched down before him so we were face to face. I pulled his gun out of his hand. "Are you Anstruther?" I asked.

He gaped at me. His walrus moustache quivered. His lip trembled. "You're British!" he said.

I shoved the gun into my waistband. "Crawl away from me," I said. "Let them see you're unarmed."

"I only fired into the air," he said. "Why did you stop me? How did you know?"

I pushed him away.

The crowd surged towards him. "I'm going for help," I said to a man behind me. "Hold him till I get the police." The man let me pass.

I had seen Lucy in the crowd, or thought I had. Also, I thought I had heard her cry out my name. But I could not wait to find her. I had to return to the hotel.

This would be my last chance to capture the murderess who now called herself Jane Griffin.

40. LUCY

After the noise and heat and terror of the past several minutes, the tranquil luxury of the hotel seemed almost surreal. I crossed the hotel lobby, opened the wrought iron door to the lift, and directed the attendant to take me to the second floor, silently blessing the look I'd gotten earlier at the hotel register.

A moment later, I was knocking on a door halfway down the long, carpeted hall.

Miss Nordstrom answered on my second knock. Her plain face registered surprise at the sight of me.

"Oh, why, it's Miss Earnshaw. How kind of you to drop by."

"You found Rosamund, then?" I asked.

"What?" Instead of stepping back to allow me to enter, Miss Nordstrom remained firmly planted in the doorway. "Oh—yes. Yes, it was very naughty of her to hide like that, but we found her in the end. I'm afraid that she's resting now, though." She cast a quick glance over her shoulder into the room behind her. "She was quite worn out by—"

"You can drop the act," I told her.

Miss Nordstrom's eyes widened. "Why, really, Miss Earnshaw, I don't know what you mean. Have you been out in the heat too long? I have heard that sunstroke can have quite extraordinary effects—"

I interrupted again. "Where is Rosamund? I hope you've at least had the decency to take her out of the trunk you packed her into while you were on the train. You must have drugged her last night so that she wouldn't wake up and make any noise when she was loaded off with the rest of the luggage. You pretended that she'd disappeared, but really she was a prisoner to ensure her father's compliance. You've been using his position as a diplomat to ship weapons and ammunition anywhere in the world he happened to be travelling. His position with the diplomatic service means that his baggage isn't searched. And if he happens to be bringing along some extra crates—well, you can easily give out a story about their being antiquities or rugs or ornaments or something that he's purchased in the course of his travels without raising anyone's suspicion. And Rosamund has been a hostage this whole time—all the while that you've been supposedly employed by her father—even if Rosamund herself didn't know it. It was the perfect cover. No one ever looked twice at the dowdy, timid governess. But all the time, you were right there at Rosamund's side, always with her, ready for something to 'accidentally' happen to her, in case her father ever tried to disobey orders or break away."

Miss Nordstrom's mouth twisted, her whole expression changing from prim and proper to one of furious distaste. "Little brat. The trouble she gave me, too—always poking and prying and sneaking off the moment my back was turned. She'd have deserved it if any accident had come to her. But she's only sleeping off the effects of the drug in the next room. Now—"

Her hand went to the pocket of her skirt with serpent-like speed—but I was faster.

"You didn't really think that I would come here unarmed, did you?" I raised my own Ladysmith revolver and levelled the barrel at her. "Keep your hands where I can see them and back—slowly—into the room."

Mr. Anstruther's role in today's assassination had been vital, but clearly he was also an asset to be readily disposed of if he were caught in the act and arrested. Rosamund was hostage to his compliance, but if they were willing to sacrifice her father, I didn't at all trust that Miss Nordstrom and whomever she was working for would have reason to keep Rosamund alive.

Miss Nordstrom obeyed, inching slowly backwards into the room with her hands raised, but her teeth were bared in a snarl.

"You think that what happens to me matters? You could shoot me and it would make no difference! You would still fail to stop what must be done."

"If you mean the assassination, it's already failed. Mr. Anstruther was found and tackled before he could make his shot."

Miss Nordstrom hardened her jaw and didn't speak, but for a split second, something glinted at the back of her gaze. Something like … triumph.

The realisation that dashed through me felt as though I'd just had a bucket of ice water splashed in my face. How long had it been since I'd left the plaza? Ten minutes? Probably not more, but anything might have happened in that time. Right now, Lord Lansdowne and the other officials were probably being hurried away from the danger and chaos, onto the waiting train—

I didn't have time to waste in trying to drag or threaten any more information out of Miss Nordstrom. I stepped forward and in one swift motion, brought the barrel of the gun up and struck her on the temple.

Whoever she actually was, life as a nursery governess had blunted her reaction times for combat. She didn't see the blow coming or make any motion to duck, only crumpled to the ground, unconscious.

The door to the hotel suite's bedroom was half-open, and through it I could see Rosamund lying on one of the twin beds. Her wrists and ankles were tied, and a cotton gag covered her mouth, but her eyes were open, blinking and frightened-looking.

I hurried across to her and untied her bonds—which were at least padded, I was glad to see, so that the ropes hadn't cut into her skin.

I helped her to sit up. "Can you walk?"

Rosamund was clearly groggy, and she stumbled when she first tried to stand up. But she nodded. "I think so."

I half-helped, half-carried her back through the outer room, where I glanced down at Miss Nordstrom's unconscious form. There wasn't time for me to waste in tying her up, though. Already I might be too late.

I took the key from the lock on the outer door, closed it behind us, and re-locked it once we were outside in the hall. Rosamund, still dazed, stumbled along beside me as we raced to the lift and descended into the hotel's lobby.

There, I sat Rosamund down in a corner on one of the velvet-covered chairs that was half-hidden from the rest of the lobby by the fronds of a potted palm tree. "I need you to stay here. You'll be safe. And I'll be back for you, I promise. But I have to go now."

Rosamund looked up at me, blinking, her small dark brows knitted into a frown. "Why did you come to rescue me?"

I gave her hands a quick squeeze. "I told you I liked you."

41. WATSON

I rode the wrought-iron lift to the floor of the room I occupied as Lord Harwell and let myself in with my key. Then I retraced my steps along the outside ledge, entering Jane Griffin's suite from her bedroom window. No one was there. From outside the open window came the noises of the street. The oxcarts, the crowds, the shrill cries of the merchants. The familiar cacophony. No hint that there had been an assassination attempt at the station nearby. I wondered if Holmes had been there. I thought I had seen Lucy, but I knew I could not have waited to look for either of them. The assassin had failed. Had Jane Griffin intended me to overpower Anstruther? Had she thought I would lose? No matter. The one thing I was certain of was that she would be returning to take the money. If not—

I had no alternative at the moment. I would play out the hand. I wondered what Clegg would do. I expected he would come back with Jane Griffin. I hefted Anstruther's gun.

42. LUCY

The scene back at the train station had settled down to one of controlled chaos, with officials in both army and police uniforms attempting to herd people away from the plaza.

I couldn't see any signs of injuries among the bystanders or evidence that anyone had been shot. But my stomach dropped at the thought of trying to find Holmes and Watson again in the crowds.

I pushed my way through, nearly colliding with a newspaper reporter who was trying to fold up the battered-looking tripod of his camera.

"Where are Lord Lansdowne and the others?" I asked breathlessly.

I had to repeat the question three times before he heard me, but finally he gestured, jerking a thumb over one shoulder. "Train platform. They're to leave at once, so I heard."

I had a stitch in my side from running by the time I reached the platform. An entire carriage had been reserved for Lord Lansdowne's party, cordoned off with red and gold tasselled ropes. My breath went out in a rush of relief at the sight of Holmes, standing just behind them.

Holmes was nearer to the train than I was, and Lord Lansdowne and a cluster of the other delegates were just about to mount the step into the carriage.

"The plate bombs!" I shouted across to Holmes.

I hadn't any proof. But at the moment, there was no time to verify my theory.

Holmes took my meaning at once, instantly diving under the ropes. He knocked Lord Lansdowne and one of the other delegates aside, and I lost sight of him for a moment behind the other onlookers. My heart jolted to a stop as I, too, ran forwards—although a voice in the back of my mind that sounded suspiciously like Holmes commented that it was surely the height of illogic to run towards a bomb.

But then I saw Holmes on the ground, with a fistful of wires in one hand.

Lord Lansdowne was peering down at him in astonishment. "Mr. Holmes, what on earth—"

Despite being on the ground, coated with dirt and dust, and having narrowly escaped death about five seconds before, Holmes answered as calmly as though he were delivering a criminology lecture at a college. "There was a bomb underneath the carriage step that would have exploded when you set foot upon it. However, you may now proceed in safety; it has been defused."

43. WATSON

Inside Jane Griffin's room all was silent.

I was behind the bedroom door, looking through the small gap at the edge of the frame into the sitting room.

I waited.

Then Jane Griffin returned, followed by Clegg. She looked rumpled from the crowd. His black wig was gone and his blonde and close-cropped hair visible once again. "I want my share," he said.

"I didn't hear an explosion," she replied.

"The timer is set for three. Fifteen minutes before departure. They'll be boarding the train."

She looked at the small table clock. "It's three now."

"Just a matter of when the first one steps up. I say it's time for us to leave."

"Payment's in my bedroom. I'll get it."

"I'm coming with you."

Their eyes were on the bed as they entered, so they did not see me behind the door. I took out Anstruther's gun in case they did.

She took the leather valise from behind the pillow and placed it on the centre of the bed. Their backs were to me.

Clegg said, "I'll watch you open it, thank you very much."

"Not sure what's in there?" She sounded almost playful.

"Not that I don't trust you, but I don't trust you."

"All right then, *you* open it."

"No, you open it," he said.

She leaned forward. Flicked the two brass hasps. Opened the top of the valise. Said, "You see?"

"I see a lot of banknotes and a gun."

"Take the money. Leave the gun."

"All right, step back."

As she did so, his arm swept around in a wide arc and I saw the gleam of a large knife blade in his hand.

He drove the blade between her shoulder blades, up to the hilt.

She gave a little gasp of surprise. Then she crumpled to the floor, her creme-coloured dress now blossoming red.

Clegg watched her for a moment. Then he stretched out his hand, reaching for the valise.

"Clegg," I said.

He turned and saw my pistol. He grinned.

"Is that Anstruther's gun? That's all right, then. Only loaded with blanks."

I did not believe him. I fired. The sound echoed inside the room.

He stood, smiling.

"Anstruther was just a distraction, you see. The real fun should start any moment now."

I fired again. The pin clicked on an empty cylinder.

Clegg took a crouching step towards me. "Did the army teach you to fight, doctor?"

But then came the loud crack of a revolver, just as loud as mine had been.

Clegg froze, and then straightened, twisting his torso and looking round to see what had hit him.

Alongside the bed, on the floor, Jane Griffin was sitting up. Both her hands clutched the silver-coated pistol. She fired again. The top of Clegg's head came off.

She smiled. A horrible, ghastly, ironic, satisfied smile.

Then she said, "God, but this hurts." Pink froth came from between her lips.

"I can help you," I said. "I'm a doctor."

"Don't touch me," she said.

Then her head lolled to the side, and the gun fell from her lifeless fingers. It made a soft thud as it hit the carpeted floor.

I touched her neck and found no pulse.

44. WATSON

I put Anstruther's gun into Clegg's hand, closed up the valise, and climbed with it through the window onto the ledge. From Harwell's room I walked down the corridor. I heard the metallic clank and whine of the lift coming up, so I took the wide marble steps. Two flights down I passed the rising lift cage. I could see a Turkish policeman behind the wrought iron bars. He was looking upwards. He did not see me.

At the lobby desk I caught the attention of the clerk. He saw the hundred-lira note in my hand.

"I wonder, do you have a Mr. Sherlock Holmes registered here?" I asked.

The man consulted his records and looked up. "For what purpose do you inquire about Mr. Holmes?"

"I have an important medical meeting with him." I lifted the valise. "The name is Watson. Dr. John H. Watson."

"You are a guest in the hotel, I believe."

I nodded.

"I see Mr. Holmes's key is here, so he is not in his room."

I nodded again. "I wonder if I might wait there." I handed him the hundred-lira note.

"He was asking for you earlier this afternoon," the clerk said as he handed me the key. "Mr. Holmes and the young woman."

45. LUCY

Night had fallen by the time we returned to the Pera Palace, fatigued and as yet having no clue as to Watson's whereabouts. He seemed to have vanished in the crowd. Had Sonnebourne's people been watching? Was he a prisoner again?

At the hotel desk, the clerk handed us our room keys. Then he said, "Mr. Holmes, your doctor came by earlier asking for you. A medical appointment? I gave him the key to your room."

I went with Holmes.

He unlocked the door and pushed it part way open. Something moved behind the window curtain.

Holmes called out, "Watson?"

The curtain moved again and Watson, wide-eyed and quivering with emotion, stepped from behind, holding a valise. "Holmes. Lucy. So good—hiding, you see—didn't mean to alarm—thought you might—"

"—might be the police?" Holmes stepped forward and put his arm around Watson's shoulder. "No need to worry about that, old friend. Mycroft has cleared your name. No more photographs in the papers. No one is looking for you."

"Except us," I said, giving him a hug.

He blushed furiously.

SATURDAY, JULY 16

46. WATSON

Holmes, Lucy and I departed from Constantinople Saturday afternoon, bound for Calais on a special train chartered from Wagons-Lits by the British Embassy. The dining car was reserved for us, and each of us had a private sleeping compartment. The train also had its own British military guard. Bandits had sometimes been encountered in the mountains, and Her Majesty's Government wished to ensure safe arrival of the valise and its contents.

Before supper was served, we spent some time in the lounge car, going over the past events. I gave my account. Holmes and Lucy each gave theirs, with Lucy adding that the British diplomat Anstruther had been reunited with his daughter. Mycroft would argue for lenience at his trial, Holmes said, in exchange for information about Sonnebourne's organisation and the Kaiser's plans to incite revolution and bloodshed in various parts of the Empire. Mrs. Torrance would soon be buried under the name of Jane Griffin.

"What next?" Lucy asked.

Holmes was silent for a long time.

Finally, he turned to me. "Sonnebourne's loyal henchman Clegg might have returned that valise, old friend. If you had not been there to stop him."

"Glad I was," I said.

"The Kaiser will want his money back," Lucy said.

"Sonnebourne's organisation will feel the pain," Holmes said. "Our long pursuit of Mrs. Torrance has ended with a good result."

"Glad of that, too," I said.

"What made you go to her room?" Holmes asked.

"I had seen her pack the money into the valise. I knew she would return for it."

"But why did you see her do that?"

"Because I was there."

At Holmes's exasperated look, Lucy intervened. "He means, why didn't you go directly to the railway station—"

"—when she said I had ordered you to stop the assassin," Holmes added. "Why did you turn back?"

"Because I knew you had given no such order."

"But she and Sonnebourne both said she was working for me."

"But I knew she was not."

"How did you know that?"

Once again, I went over the chain of reasoning in my mind.

Shoot the Torrance woman, Sonnebourne had said to the man seated on the other side of his desk. *She is working for Holmes.*

I now knew the man to have been Clegg. But Clegg did not recognise her by that name. And Sonnebourne expected that, for he had been prepared with a photograph of the woman.

Therefore, Sonnebourne's name for the woman had not been intended for Clegg to hear. It had been intended for me to *overhear.*

Therefore, Sonnebourne was lying. Therefore, the Torrance woman was *not* working for Holmes.

The Torrance woman is your answer.

Holmes and Lucy were looking at me expectantly.

Would I tell them what really had happened? Would I reveal that I had dreamed of Holmes floating cross-legged above my bed, on cushions, twice telling me that the Torrance woman was my answer? And that I only realised what he meant while clinging to the roof of the Orient Express, after midnight, during a lightning-storm?

"Let us just say," I replied, "that I know your methods."

Holmes's brow shot upwards, but only for a moment.

THE END

HISTORICAL NOTE

This is a work of fiction, and the authors make no claim that any of the historical locations or historical figures appearing in this story had even the remotest connection with the adventures recounted herein. However ...

1. The Orient Express was begun in 1883 by the Compagnie Internationale des Wagons-Lits, which continues to operate as an international hotel and travel logistics company. The route of the original Orient Express train service changed many times. Travelers today can ride in original CIWL carriages (from the 1920s and 1930s) on the Venice-Simplon Orient Express train, from Victoria Station in London to Venice and to other destinations in Europe, including the original route from Paris to Constantinople (now Istanbul).

2. The Pera Palace Hotel was built in 1892 to accommodate wealthy travelers, particularly those arriving in Constantinople on the Orient Express. Begun by the Wagons-Lits Company, it continues to operate as a luxury destination to this date. The hotel maintains Room 411 as the Agatha Christie Room, with original antique furniture, books, and an authentic period typewriter in honor of the famed author, who is said to have written *Murder on the Orient Express* while staying there as a guest. The hotel elevator with the wrought iron cab that appears in our story continues to operate.

3. As a fan tribute, the little girl whom Lucy befriends during their journey is named Rosamund, after Agatha Christie's real-life daughter.

4. The Convention of Constantinople, a treaty regulating the use of the Suez Canal, was signed in Constantinople in 1888 by the United Kingdom, France, and other European powers as well as the Russian and Ottoman Empires. Britain and France disputed the extent of England's powers under the treaty, a disagreement that was not resolved until the Entente Cordiale in 1904.

5. The Müşir Ahmet Paşa Station, now renamed as the Sirkeci Railway station, continues to operate in Istanbul, though it no longer serves as the terminus for international express train lines. The other historic sites mentioned in our story continue to be enjoyed by thousands of visitors every year.

6. Lucy James will return.

A NOTE OF THANKS
TO OUR READERS

Thank you for reading this Sherlock and Lucy story. We hope you've enjoyed it.

As you probably know, reviews make a big difference! So, we also hope you'll consider going back to the Amazon page where you bought the story and uploading a quick review. You can get to that page by clicking on this link to our website and scrolling down:

sherlockandlucy.com/project/watson-on-the-orient-express
(bit.ly/3b3cdgj)

You can also sign up for our mailing list to receive updates on new stories, special discounts, and 'free days' for some of our other books: www.SherlockandLucy.com

ABOUT THE AUTHORS

Anna Elliott is the author of the *Twilight of Avalon* trilogy, and *The Pride and Prejudice Chronicles*. She was delighted to lend a hand in giving the character of Lucy James her own voice, firstly because she loves Sherlock Holmes as much as her father, Charles Veley, and second because it almost never happens that someone with a dilemma shouts, "Quick, we need an author of historical fiction!" She lives in Pennsylvania with her husband and four children.

Charles Veley is the author of the first two books in this series of fresh Sherlock Holmes adventures. He is thrilled to be contributing Dr. Watson's chapters for the series, and delighted beyond words to be collaborating with Anna Elliott.